ALSO BY T.E. MACARTHUR

From TreasureLine Books & Publishing

The Volcano Lady: Volume I – A Fearful Storm Gathering (2011)
The Volcano Lady: Volume II – To the Ending of the World (2012)

The Yankee Must Die: Huaka'i Po (the Nightmarchers) (2013)
The Yankee Must Die: Death and the Barbary Coast (2013)

From Q-werks Design
Shamanka: Oracle of the Shamaness (2008)

From The Tarot Media Company
Shamanka: Oracle of the Shamaness Guidebook (2011)

WORDS OF PRAISE FOR *THE GASLIGHT ADVENTURES OF TOM TURNER*:

"T.E. does a phenomenal job of bringing to life the era of the Merry Monarch, King Kalakaua, and, as an added bonus, the original 'Volcano Lady', Madame Pele herself... Our Yankee hero, Tom, is a wonderful rogue that you root for every step of the way, especially since from the very first page he's facing a cliffhanger of mammothly oxygen-deprived proportions"
~ Penelope Dreadfulle, author & blogger

"T. E. MacArthur really has a knack for creating entertaining historical fiction. ... she puts Tom Turner (a major character in the Volcano Lady series) center stage for a real "penny dreadful" adventure... There are lots of twists, turns, clever steampunk-ish inventions and more in this adventure tale."
~ Sharon E. Cathcart, author of In the *Eye of the Beholder* and *His Beloved Infidel.*

"A wild ride with the <u>Victorian Jason Bourne</u>... This modern "penny dreadful" was a fast, exciting read, full of all the thrills and chills you would expect from the genre."
~ "Davispigeon", Amazon Reviewer

THE YANKEE MUST DIE

THE GASLIGHT ADVENTURES OF TOM TURNER

TERROR IN A WILD WEIRD WEST

BY
T.E. MACARTHUR

The Yankee Must Die:
The Gaslight Adventures of Tom Turner
Terror in a Wild Weird West
By T.E. MacArthur

©2013 by T.E. MacArthur
Edition 1.0 (2013)

Cover Artwork/Design: S. N. Jacobson
        www.snjacobson.com
Published by: TreasureLine Publishing (never mind the cover saying Gaslight Adventure Books and Publishing)
        www.TreasureLinePublishing.com

ISBN 13: 978-1-61752-165-2
ISBN 10: 1-61752-165-5

Also available in eBook publication and paperback
www.volcanolady1.wordpress.com
www.TreasureLineBooks.com

The following is a work of fiction. Names, characters, places, and incidents are fictitious or used fictitiously. Any resemblance to real persons, living or dead, to factual events or to businesses is coincidental and unintentional.

Printed in the United States of America

*Dedicated to my **Mother** and to my **Papa** as always.*

Unbelievably huge thanks to **Laura Ehrlich**, **Brandy Sluss**, and **Penelope Dreadfulle** (aka Dover Whitcliff) for their opinions and editing skills – along with quite a bit of cheerleading!

*To Monsieur **Jules Verne**, the Father of Science Fiction (and Steampunk!)*

Many thanks to the bewildering number of people who kept me sane and on track: **Alex MacIver; Roy Nonomura; Jay Davis; Juliana and Patrick Gaul; My pals Sharon E. Cathcart, Scott Perkins, Elizabeth Watasin, and Maggie Secara; Molly Burke** (the Queen of Confidence); **Dennis Kytasaari** (NAJVS); **Penelope Anne Bartotto** (the Book Review Mama herself); and **David Batzloff.** To my best cheerleaders **Adam and Karin Mckechnie-Lid.**

To the wonderful members of the <u>Steam Federation – Bay Area Steampunk Association</u>. Most especially **Gene Forrer**, who inspired the character of Albert Forrer in Yankee #1 and provided invaluable technical knowledge on dirigibles, locomotives, traction, and fueling of the period.

To **Patrick James (PJ) Lacy** for introducing me to Texas John Slaughter and an array of details on life in the Wild West.

To the owners and tour guides at the <u>Bird Cage Theater</u> in Tombstone Arizona who kindly gave me a backstage tour and some fascinating history.

To the brilliant designer of the cover: **Stephen Jacobson** (<u>www.snjacobson.com</u>).

To the continuing and inspiring resources: the <u>U.S. Naval Landing Party</u> (Civil War Naval Re-enactors) and the <u>North American Jules Verne Society</u> (NAJVS.)

To **Linda Boulanger** and the gang at **TreasureLine Books and Publishing**

Freezing water.

Death had been chasing Tom Turner and had now caught up. His fingertips went numb. So too did his feet. His lungs burned. There was little difference between this and being strangled ... hanged ... he knew what a hanging felt like.

... It was over ...

His life ... oh God what a life he'd led ...

Early March 1884 (one month <u>earlier</u>)
Office of the Marshal
Truckee, Nevada

The little man rubbed his sore head with one hand and wadded up the telegram with the other. It was entirely intolerable. While certain necessary funds were being arranged from far away in France, he had to sit in the jail cell smelling over-boiled coffee and heaven only knew what else. His jailors hadn't even bothered to bring him a new bandage. Not that the injury was particularly threatening, but there were certain things he felt were his due.

They laughed at him.

The place was so dirty.

And it was cold.

Cairo pushed the broken pair of wire-rimmed spectacles back into his pocket. It was dreadful; he could barely read with them, let alone without them. He'd have to get a new pair and they were very expensive. It was that Turner fellow's fault. He'd tricked him, taken his lovely guns, and tossed Cairo from the train. The awful Yankee had actually hit him!

He tried combing his sandy-colored hair with his hand and occasionally stopped to take a sniff of his perfume scented cuff – it had some lingering perfume on it. Nothing helped. It was intolerable.

He, known as *the Egyptian* on account of his family name, was one of Pierre-Jules Hetzel's finest, most effective agents.

The telegram was compressed into a wrinkled ball and suddenly the Egyptian was horrified that he'd caused such chaos in such a small form. Carefully, he unfolded the paper and smoothed it out over his knee.

Truckee Marshal's Office

Mr. Heinrich Cairo, temporarily incarcerated

Whereabouts of Yankee acknowledged. Do not continue pursuit. New agent in route. Bail arrangements underway. Return to Paris immediately.

P. J. Hetzel, Publisher

Paris, France

Intolerable. He had only had a single setback, and Hetzel was already sending his replacement. Heaven only knew who that was. Certainly not so clever a man as Cairo thought himself to be.

Still, it did not show his loyalty to so egregiously attack the communication from his esteemed employer. Pierre Jules Hetzel was one of France's most revered citizens. Publisher, patriot, and patron of French society. Hetzel was more than that: he was the designer behind a network of intelligence collectors and mechanically enhanced men. Cairo considered himself the finer of the first category and was relieved by the sheer fact he was not a bio-mechanic agent in the second category.

It had been Hetzel who had created Cairo's moniker, the Egyptian, which Cairo found very flattering. It made him sound exotic and grandiose. It lent gravitas to his otherwise diminutive physical stature and mundane appearance. He wasn't entirely disappointed he did not live up to the moniker, neither being so impressive nor even Egyptian in origin: there was value to not drawing attention to one's self – to blending in – to fooling those into thinking he was not a threat.

Tom Turner had fallen for Cairo's false exterior. Cairo had entirely planned on using this advantage against the man, but luck had not prevailed. Even holding Turner at gunpoint had not stopped the vulgar Yankee from … what did they call it … sucker punching him. It was unsporting and infuriating. And it hurt.

So, Turner remained on the train headed east while Cairo was stuck in some unknown town, in a jail cell. And Hetzel had already replaced him. Surely he had not entirely failed, he had reported where the Yankee was headed and had a much better understanding of how the man thought.

The more he thought about it, the angrier Cairo became. It was not fair. Not at all. His reputation might be sullied to the point of not being useful for further employment. The Egyptian pulled himself into a tighter ball, as if the filth of the cell would not be able to get to him. He would be free soon. He had to prove himself again to Hetzel. And he would, as he knew what no other agent could know: he understood Turner on a deeper level of philosophy. Yes, he would complete his original mission. And if not, he knew how to secure "other arrangements."

He liked the sweet smoke of a cheroot but actually detested the smell of regular cigars. It did not please him to find his cheap room filled with a veil of pungent, regular cigar stench.

That was the least of his worries. He was either in grave danger or about to embarrass himself profoundly. Now he was clinging to his revolver like a child holds a blanket, with approximately the same emotional attachment.

The red-headed man stood waiting, mildly annoyed and equally impressed. A military man. Tall. Bearded. A tad unkempt. Familiar.

Turner knew the face. "Sir?" He was staring at General William Tecumseh Sherman, Commanding General of the United States Army ...

"Turner? It's about time we met."

... the general who saved him from death in Andersonville Prison.

"Don't sailors talk? I'm told army men can't shut up – well, perhaps they just meant me." The man had a twinkle in his hazel eyes, now that they weren't wondering what might happen with the gun that had been pointed at him.

"General?" Turner found one appropriate word.

"Good. You know two words. Think you can produce a sentence? How about an answer?"

"To what question, sir?"

"Where the hell do you keep the whiskey? Two men shouldn't sit and talk of old times without something to drink. Old times *and* new times. I think you may have some interesting new times ahead of you."

The Turner Luck held true.

Along with feeling he'd finally beaten Hetzel, now he was getting a long held wish fulfilled. His world could not have been better in that moment. It was a sign that his life had turned a corner and would be just fine. "General Sherman?"

"It's an easy question, son. Where do you keep the whiskey? I have some harder questions, and you might want a drink before you have to answer them." Sherman's expression changed from amused to concerned. "You *do* have whiskey, or bourbon, or something, don't you?"

A laugh slipped out of Turner; more of an uncontrolled bark in surprise and relief. "Under the table there, at the window. It's not mine and I don't necessarily want to know how it got there."

"You mean it was in reach all the time?" The General stuck his cigar in his mouth, dropped his hat and coat onto the rocker by the window, and began rummaging under the table.

"They don't believe in glassware, sir."

"Well, if you don't mind, I don't. Had to share a bottle more than once. Grant was sort of funny about it, but then he didn't drink half as much as anyone said he did. Good man, Grant – stood by me when I was crazy, I stood by him when he was drunk. Of course, I wasn't insane nor was he soused. Those were some interesting days."

"Commanding General of the U.S. Army?" Turner was still incredulous.

"Soon to retire," Sherman corrected, the words spoken around his cigar. A moment later he stood up, having found the necessary bottle.

"Sir, I ... I ..."

"Relax, son. I'm not here to pester you about your prior employment as Robur's first mate on a flying clipper ship. Not my orders. Besides, there are far worse things to worry over than one errant sailor."

Turner quickly put away the revolver. It seemed beyond rude to be armed in the presence of a man he admired – and owed his life to.

The cork took some effort to get out and Sherman was disappointed to discover that the bottle was half empty. He took a sip. He was the guest and would be expected to drink first. Besides, he was too curious to know if the whiskey was any good. It wasn't. Perfect, he thought. As he lowered the bottle and offered it to Turner, he got a good look at the naval man's famous scar.

Turner accepted the bottle and in his usual, well-practiced way, cut off any view of his disfigurement. He sized up Sherman quickly. The General was dressed in civilian attire, though if that was to conceal his presence in Denver, it was a wasted effort. Sherman's appearance graced many photographic collections, filled newspapers, and was generally recognizable. He was not average in his looks by any means. The red hair was a giveaway too. Dangling by a polished gold chain was a watch, sequestered in its pocket, and a fob with the photograph and hair of a woman. Sherman's rather famous wife? His *second* wife but that was another story in itself – for a much different time, though admittedly, Turner was curious.

Sherman was quite the sight and must have been simply amazing to view, with sixty-five thousand men following him through the South and up the East Coast. His men had been suitably impressed and they loved him still, calling him "Uncle Billy."

Turner had never actually seen him in person before this.

Sherman's men may have freed the prisoners of Andersonville, like Turner, but the man himself had been more centrally located amongst his troops toward the north, directing the most brazen wartime operation in history. Hannibal and Alexander had nothing on Sherman, or so Turner thought. He was biased on the subject though, as the rescue of Union prisoners had spared his life. Standing there, drinking with the man, Turner wasn't sure if he should be worshiping at the man's feet or slapping him on the shoulder like an old wartime comrade.

"Sir, I ... why *are* you here?"

"Specifically to meet you."

"Whatever for?"

"We want you back."

As the words sank in, Turner had to sit down on the edge of the bed. He drank deeply this time. "I have to ask the question again, whatever for?"

Sherman took the bottle, drank, and sat down in the rocker. "As you know too well, things aren't what they used to be. Hell, spies and saboteurs have been replaced with mechanical monstrosities and madmen. No one wants to take their neighbor's farm anymore, they want to take over the whole world. Our government isn't always able to respond to such threats. It isn't always able to acknowledge them, if you understand my meaning?"

"You want Robur's inventions." Turner was suddenly very disappointed. He had dared to hope that his country might want him back because he was a good man, a veteran, an "honest sailor" as Dr. Lettie Gantry had called him.

"I'd love to have them, but unless I want everyone else having them too, it's better that none of us do." Sherman swallowed a gulp of whiskey that comfortably burned down the inside of his throat, cutting through dust and dirt in the air. "We need you back because you understand the men who make those abominations. And, you have firsthand knowledge of the latest, substantial threats. God knows the country's always in some sort of danger, but with this new threat? For once, I don't think we can just laugh it off. You took on this … Confederacy nonsense single handedly." He took a long draw on his cigar, watching Turner intensely. "And you did a rather fine job sneaking around for us during the war. How could we not want someone with your skills back in the fold?"

"I failed, rather sublimely at one point." Turner unconsciously shifted his collar over his scar.

"So did I! Spectacularly and frequently. Made every damn paper in the country, each and every time I failed. But here I am. And here you are."

Turner looked at his hands, which were getting scarred with wear and age. "If I should choose to agree, don't you think some of your colleagues will be uncomfortable serving with a …" He couldn't find the words. He was no turncoat, never a traitor, yet he had walked away from his native country to fly around the world with Robur. And Robur had been a rogue, flying free across borders and threatening the status quo of civilization.

"… a veteran left to starve in the streets?" Sherman's voice rose. "Worst damn thing we ever did! Good men, solid men. Men who gave limbs to the cause of holding this country together. What did we do? We shook their hands, patted them on the back, and sent them packing with barely a penny. And not everyone had a place to go."

That seemed such an honest admission from Sherman. He had a reputation for giving his last cent to any man who claimed to have marched to the sea with him and now needed help. But then, he also had a reputation for acts of war that shook every rule of engagement to its core and teetered on the edge of barbarism. The man was a walking testament to complication. How *his* men were treated once the fighting stopped was clearly a sore subject. He changed it quickly. "Truth is; we're damned scared. You and I, we both know there's no glory in war. But how do you fight an enemy that's in love with war, always looking for that great battle that will bring back lost honor from the past? In light of the recent events at Fort Point, we thought it might be good to contact you right away. To reach you long before you tried for the east. I'm not sure you left too many friends back in California."

Turner nodded. "You do realize that certain recent events, had nothing to do with a possible war. There are some *situations* I'm not sure you are aware of yet that go beyond what happened with the New Confederacy. *I'm* not a particularly safe man to be around – this is one reason why I have few friends. Simply being near me is enough to put your life in danger. Why would the Administration send its top General into such a dangerous situation? You are at risk here, sir."

"A loner, eh?" Sherman drank for a fairly long time. His shoulders dropped and he slumped back into the rocking chair. "I'm not here on behalf of the Administration. I'm here because a group of foolish *old men* think they can use their geriatric experience to save the world - starting with our own country. While you'd technically be back in the Navy, you'd be reporting directly to us. Call it a permanent loan from the War Department."

Nothing is ever straight forward, is it, Turner thought with disappointment.

"You wouldn't be acting out there completely alone, Turner. That's something I think you've done for too long … or maybe thought you had to. Not true. I assure you that you will not be out in the wind. But the President and Congress need to claim ignorance."

"When haven't they?"

"Well, true, but this is by design – they don't *want* to know what is going on. Active or retired, I will stand by any orders I give you and I'll stand with you. We all will. We've been in that position: some of us were abandoned to the press and the mob. None of us will let that happen again."

Turner reached out for the bottle. Sherman allowed him to have it … slowly. Turner looked back into the intense stare Sherman was giving him. "Who, may I ask, are 'we'?"

"Can I take it you're signing up?"

"Not necessarily. I've leapt too often without looking. I'd like to be sure of what I'm signing up for. *You* have the reputation, but do your partners?"

Sherman had been leaning far forward in the chair, but now pushed back and kept looking at Turner. This was the leap of faith he knew he might have to take. "I think you can appreciate that I cannot expose our ... gentleman's society."

"And I think that you can appreciate that I need to know what I'm getting into. The last set of men who wanted my help called themselves a gentleman's club too. Then they tried to kill me."

"Are you saying 'no'?"

"I'm saying 'maybe,' sir. I understand the need for discretion. I can offer you this: I'm in no position to advance my cause at your expense.

For a long time, neither man chose to comment. The bottle simply kept being passed back and forth. They watched each other for signs.

A leap of faith. "Grant is among us."

"Sir?"

"Former President Grant. A couple of naval scientists. Edison too, though a bit reluctantly. And the one man you might know from your naval career: Admiral David Porter."

"Good God." Turner swallowed a long, large gulp of the whiskey, taking the contents down to the last. "Admiral Porter himself agreed to this?"

Sherman only nodded.

"I wouldn't have thought he'd put up with it. With me."

"Why not? You didn't entirely break any American laws with ... what was his name? Robur. Did you?" Sherman was sometimes hard to read, whether or not he was being playful or serious.

"I think I shouldn't say. But I believe Admiral Porter is not fond of anyone who diverges from the rank and file. He might be the first and foremost man bothered by my former activities."

"Not sure he knows you very well, Turner. Seems he's just as mystified by you as the rest of us are. But he concluded you were the right man for the job."

"Are you mystified? You should have doubts."

"Not after you brought down that Confederate airship." Sherman thought for a moment or two, and then ran his hand through his reddish hair, making it more unkempt than before. "I don't know. But to be honest, I can be an immovable, opinionated bastard when I want to be. Yet ... yet a man who doesn't make any mistakes worries me more. I'll tell you, if you ever find newspapers from '61, especially from Ohio or New York, you'd hear all about how General Sherman was insane. And, at the time, I think I might have been. I saw Confederates and monstrous weapons coming out of every street corner and grove. Hell and damnation, I swear to this day I saw a mechanical man some six stories tall. Some sort of steam-powered man. Everyone doubted me. I doubted me. I ..." He took the last of the whiskey. "I lost my mind for a bit. Did things I normally wouldn't, but at the time they seemed right; even sane." He pushed away the memory of standing on his father-in-law's back acreage with a loaded pistol, pointing it at his own temple, ready to pull the trigger – a vile newspaper lying at his feet. Whatever hand of heaven reached down and kept him from committing suicide that day in complete disgrace had also given him a new chance on life. "It would be disingenuous of me not to give good men a second chance. That's what I'm doing here. Things are getting dicey. Will you consider our proposal?"

"I will, sir. I will say nothing of your colleagues no matter which way I choose. It would be disingenuous of me not to believe that what you are doing is honorable. The chance to have a part in some of that honor is tempting." Turner considered what the General had said for a moment. "Don't dismiss the New Confederacy – there are more of them than I saw and I suspect the organization to be far larger than is known. Add the Prussians and possibly the Spanish? You say you're scared, so am I. Oh, and sir, turns out you were right about the steam men."

"I was?" He seemed genuinely surprised, then relieved. "We need more whiskey."

The lecture hall was absolutely full. It galled Professor Ashfield, Dean of the College, that most if not all were there to listen to someone else's lecture. He couldn't believe that his theory of fluid rock formation was being surpassed if not entirely ignored. It was not only brilliant scholarship on his part, but Biblically supported and supporting, which was his purpose in proposing it. While learned men early in the century had claimed that all sedimentary rock had been formed during Noah's Great Flood less than 10,000 years ago, others argued that the Earth was ageless and therefore the rocks were ancient beyond calculation. Ashfield straddled the two and found common ground that didn't seem to resolve anything the way he thought it should: surely it was obvious that the Great Flood had created all sedimentary rock but that the Earth was a bit older than 10,000 years? He personally calculated it at 84,237 years old.

But, *she* was fire to his water.

She produced mathematical proofs for an older Earth, more than 100 million years old, more than a ridiculous one billion years. She produced hypotheses that showed landmasses commonly held to be sedimentary were actually volcanically created. Well, those hypotheses would be cut down by greater intellects, but until then, she would be a celebrity. And worst of all, she was a very good speaker … for a woman … and she made him appear bland, sterile, and ignorant. She'd not done it on purpose, oh no, of course not, but he knew she secretly harbored resentment toward him for blocking her from joining the faculty of the College. It was unnatural for a woman to be lecturing … in public! Women did not have the brain capacity that men had – that was scientifically proven - and therefore by nature could not comprehend the complex logic of mathematics. Women were emotional creatures, prone to life-ruining mistakes and needed to be reined in – controlled – assisted – guided. They had no place teaching at universities. Oh, how she must hate him for reminding her of her weakness and folly. A woman geologist … a female tragedy!

Ashfield folded his arms and pretended not to be listening.

The applause when she was announced was mixed. Some did not offer an enthusiastic clap in case they might be caught giving their approval to a freak of nature. Most, however, had been there before and were eagerly awaiting her lecture. If it concerned her that she was not fully accepted by the men in the lecture hall, she did not show it, having the proper manners to hide anything she might do or say that might disturb a gentleman.

One fellow sat near the back. He too was watching Lettie carefully. Dr. John Watson had made himself reasonably informed on the subject of volcanoes so that he could both enjoy her lecture and yet be free to examine the audience for the man or men who threatened her life. It galled him that any woman was so threatened. It was outrageous!

As the welcome died down and Dr. Lettie Gantry, Volcanologist, took to the lectern, Watson began a systematic search of the seated attendees. Her would-be assassin could easily be tucked into the shadows. Was that her neighbor, Miranda Gray, seated in the back? He hoped so. Dr. Gantry could likely use cheerful support.

"Good evening. And thank you for your kind welcome, again." Lettie's voice was a tad husky, made worse by the time spent breathing toxic fumes gushing from tears in the Earth's surface. She knew how to hold her audience by topic, presentation, and general appearance. She understood that she was an alien amongst the men in the room and used many of the social norms she flaunted usually to her advantage. The epitome of simple, feminine fashion, she wore a tailored suit with a small bustle, in dark blue wool. Nothing ridiculous in ornament, yet expensive in texture – at once declaring that she was of excellent breeding while not being outlandish.

The audience accepted it.

Dr. John Watson admired it. Sherlock Holmes would have dismissed it as a case of female manipulation … all the while silently appreciating her skills.

"In light of such developments in the East Indies, it is necessary that we put the eruption of Krakatoa in perspective. Tonight, we will discuss the Lakagígar or the Craters of Laki eruption of 1783 and 1784, comparing and contrasting the fissure eruption in

Iceland with information observed this year at Krakatoa. We may also cite the publication of a popularist biography by Monsieur Jules Verne, a 'Journey to the Center of the Earth'," she lifted her hand to cover a laugh she was withholding, "in dispelling many entertaining but entirely impossible notions about the nature of volcanic eruptions and our current understanding of the interior of the Earth."

That sounds promising, Watson thought as he concluded his initial observations of the audience. It was his fifth Gantry lecture, and thus far she had made the dull and bland sound quite exciting.

"As has been noted in earlier discussions, Krakatoa was a complex volcano, often classified as a stratovolcano." Lettie would occasionally look down at her notes, but rarely for more than a second, and then she would look directly at members of the audience with her marvelously green eyes. "The Laki eruption was quite different. On the 8th of June, 1783, a series of fissures opened up on either side of the Laki Mountain in southwest Iceland, and produced some of the most significant lava flows in recorded history. Upward of one hundred and thirty craters erupted an estimated fourteen square kilometers of basalt lavas. This was the least of the threats generated by the eruption, which coincided with another Icelandic eruption of the Grímsvötn volcano. All totalled, the gases and ash emitted during the two years was substantial, and traces have been found as far away as Germany and Russia. This eruption ..."

She stopped, her eyes wide, staring at one man in the third row.

Watson leaned forward but couldn't see the man clearly.

For a long moment, everyone wondered if she'd lost her place or was succumbing to feminine weakness under the pressure of public scrutiny. Good God, would she faint?

Watson knew better. Dr. Gantry had come to him and his odd rooming partner, Sherlock Holmes, to seek their assistance. Holmes, much to Watson's disapproval, had dismissed her fears for some Yank in America and for herself as being the result of womanly hysteria. He'd looked into her story and chosen not to take her case. Watson recalled the fury he'd turned on his friend and the promise he'd then made to protect her from whatever threat she perceived.

Damn it, he couldn't see the man she was looking at.

As suddenly as she'd stalled in her lecture, Lettie brightened up and began again as though nothing was bothering her. Now, that was the Dr. Gantry he'd come to admire.

"… this eruption was chemically, physically, and destructively different from Krakatoa, providing us with a significant example arguing against a commonality between all eruptions. Let us begin with a comparative summary of the two types of volcanic eruption. We will then discuss the nature of *the direct threat to human life*," she turned her eyes to Watson with the emphasis on her words, "concluding with an understanding of the consequences of both eruptions."

For the full torturous hour, Watson tried to see who was seated in the third row. He could see the hand resting on an elegant cane, a head full of dark hair, and the unmoving gaze he kept on Dr. Gantry. Yet he could not see the man's face in any detail. Finally, the lecture ended and he, like nearly every student or journalist in the room, rushed forward. A solid wall of men blockaded him from getting to either Dr. Gantry or the man who clearly terrified her into momentary silence.

With all the arms and legs and waving hands wishing to be recognized with their question, the cause of Dr. Gantry's brief pause escaped. Watson finally fought his way to the lectern. Lettie looked to him, both angry and frightened, and mouthed the words, "he was here."

"The Elegant Man?" Watson asked, using the moniker she marked her tormentor with.

Lettie nodded.

As Watson stood beside her, observing the dangerous closeness of the third row seat the Elegant Man had been in, he noted her open reticule on the lectern shelf, a small caliber pistol's grip protruding.

Of course it was a dream. Turner had been laying there, hands supporting the back of his head, staring up at the ceiling, and watching the changes in light from the flickering candle. Turner never slept in the dark if he had the choice. Pitch dark was too much like the windowless prison cell they'd kept him in the night before his execution at Andersonville Prison Camp. It was also too dangerous: a man could be surprised by an enemy in the dark.

Sherman sent word – acting as if Turner had given a positive answer to his proposal – to join him for a little christening ceremony at the rail yard. Some political nonsense. Yet, with Turner's newly gained knowledge of the Confederate locomotive, it was possible Sherman wanted to compare that monstrosity with the latest from a Union builder. Turner hadn't said yes to rejoining the Navy ... yet. He still might not. Beyond his self doubts, there was the danger factor. Anyone near him was in peril. Alone, he could maneuver and hide, watch and plan. If he had to answer to a series of commanding officers, that might not be possible and would no doubt cost some soldier or sailor his life. No. He simply couldn't agree to go back, much as his soul begged him to.

He had dozed a bit, but the excitement of the week had both exhausted him and set his mind in motion. Rest had been fitful and broken. It occurred to him that he had a dream fulfilled, even if he couldn't pursue it. They want me back, he wondered, slightly amused.

He must have finally drifted off to a deep sleep.

This was most certainly a dream. He knew it, as he walked through scene after scene of jumbled chaos. Everyone else appeared to be unaware that they were dreaming. Just Turner. He felt strangely satisfied that he alone had an almost god-like understanding of the situation.

Could someone die in their dream? Would that kill them in reality? Turner knew he'd dreamed of his execution over and over for years – it plagued his health – yet he awoke each time. Of course, he'd survived the actual hanging, keeping only a horrible scar around his throat as a souvenir. He believed that dreams and real life had no effect on one another, but there were those who said that dreams and life were one and the same. It was too philosophical for the moment.

At first, he found himself standing at the great wheel of the airship *Albatross,* his home for a decade. A glorious clipper ship sailing through the clouds, driven by multiple lifting screws that held the craft aloft. Behind him stood his captain, Robur, arms folded across a vast chest, feet apart to brace against sudden turbulence. Jean Robur. Robur the Conqueror. Master of the air and creator of the most brilliant of all flying craft. If Turner had a sense of divine understanding, it paled in comparison to Robur's vision of the world. What a waste: Robur's intelligence had overwhelmed his sanity.

Turner looked over his shoulder at his captain. Before his eyes, the great man faded into a mass of paranoid hysteria and fear, then melted into a pile of broken bones and lacerations. Turner's hands would not free themselves from the wheel. He could not help Robur. In seconds the corpse disintegrated into dust and vanished. It was a dream, Turner reminded himself, but the feeling of loss and grief weighed heavily on him. Robur had been situated to show the world that it wasn't trapped in a cycle of war and hopelessness. What invention could Robur have made that would have led to peace and prosperity? What innovation was denied to the world because he'd gone mad and gotten himself killed? The question was one that would haunt Turner and leave him wondering if he'd failed in not saving Robur from himself.

The dust was gone. Turner's hands were suddenly freed from the wheel and he stood staring at the floor where Robur had been.

He thought he'd heard a voice. But dreams were notorious for mismatching sound and vision. He turned around to see that it was no longer the *Albatross,* but the *NCSS Albermarle II* he was standing on. A Southern abomination, created for a New Confederacy by Prussian military leaders seeking to control portions of the North American continent … and more. A flying ironclad warship: the killer of soldiers. He'd seen it in action. All those dead men at Fort Point and it was only going to get worse if the New Confederacy remained unchecked. They were gunning with new energy, confidence, and weaponry for *his country.* It was entirely possible that the Union would not survive a second war. Would a

New Confederacy be satisfied with stopping at the Mason-Dixon? They'd told him that they already planned on taking parts of Mexico and the West Coast as far north as Canada. Where would it stop?

In a swirl of images and dislocated bodies, he watched his personal laundry list of enemies sweep around him. Hetzel and his bio-mechanical army – all those poor souls kept alive by machinery he couldn't comprehend. Admiral Hagen, with his ram-rod posture and fierce loyalty to Prussia and the art of war. Milton, the Confederate who thought he'd use the Prussian nation to bring back a South that no longer existed. Poor little Heinrich Cairo, Hetzel's latest failed agent. What did they matter, he thought, walking through them? Hetzel was far away in Paris, tending to his republic and unable to best Turner with the worst machines at his disposal. Hagen had flown away in a barely operable *Albermarle*. Milton had died at the *Albermarle's* crash site. Cairo was too fussy and self-centered to be a viable threat, and Turner had thrown him off a moving train when they'd met.

In truth, it was Turner, himself, who was the greatest threat. He knew too much.

The *Albermarle* had none of the elegance or simplicity that Robur had designed into the *Albatross*. It had none of the efficiencies either, which was what made Turner's life such an ordeal. With Robur dead, there was only one living witness to his innovations and inventions. The Prussians wanted what Turner knew. The United States wanted him. The most powerful intelligencer in the French Republic, Pierre-Jules Hetzel, wanted him. The Confederates wanted him. Lettie did not.

The hand that rested on his shoulder was hers. It made all the sense in the world that he would dream about her. Lettie. Dr. Letticia Gantry, volcanologist and geologist. An academic novelty in a world that said females could not understand logic, reason, or science. A spinster technically, though he considered the notion that she married her profession. She certainly hadn't married him; he'd not had the temerity to ask. Oh, it was all so convoluted: Robur needed her expertise thus he'd ordered Turner to abduct her. Turner, following orders, had done so, with varying degrees of success and failure. Ultimately, he'd chosen to do right by Lettie, freeing her from Robur. Robur had not forgiven his betrayal.

She stood there, looking into his eyes as she had done so many times. He would always remember when they had nearly changed from acquainted to intimate. Nearly. She had not so sullied herself with the "American." Oh, but they had come so close only to be interrupted by an erupting volcano.

The scene began to smear into the next, but Lettie still stood there, her face showing all her pity and kindness. Her letter to him, saying goodbye, was kind. Of course it was. It teetered on the brink of being loving, but he'd abandoned any belief in love, in the romantic sense. And she was wise not to associate herself with a man of his reputation: a man who was nothing more than a saboteur, a kidnapper, a thief on occasion, a killer … She deserved better.

For some reason, he felt aware of his circumstances and his dreaming state. "Lucid" dreaming was what it was called? Neither deep in slumber nor awake. In control and yet not. Might he now roll over and willfully dream of what might have happened had Krakatoa not erupted?

Instead, he heard the sound of something awful. A horrible howling. An enormous dog wailing in the distance. His dream was becoming a nightmare. A regular beat, thumping in his ears, shaking his body – his own heart beat? He knew the sound. He'd heard it before.

Turner sat up.

He could hear a wagon rolling down the street but no other sounds. No howling.

He sluggishly made his way to the window, his breath producing a light billow of whitened air. The window frame leaked cold air into his room. The cheap curtain did little to block the frigid temperature. The floor beneath his bare feet was frozen.

It was snowing. Silently. Heavily.

The wagon left a trail behind it in the street, muddied by each wheel. Some poor fellow was out at this hour? Even the rail station, two blocks away, was dark and quiet. The storm might pass by morning, yet in the meantime, it laid a dense blanket of clouds over the town. Denver was a growing, thriving city, and most residents knew better than to go out in the cold.

His heart was pounding. He'd thought the haunting noise was real.

It was nothing more than a lucid dream. Perhaps the wagon and clomping steps of the horse had filled his drowsy head with the idea of a baying in the night. It was funny how those things worked – common, everyday sounds or sights distorted into fear.

What had set him off? What was it about that sound he'd dreamed?

It was too cold to stay by the window. Turner quickly climbed back under the blankets, the lingering warmth he'd left behind being nearly gone. He rolled onto his side, leaving his back to the window, and grasped his pillow against his head.

Sleep might not come so easily again. Every nerve was alert to the slightest noise. Yet, he felt foolish. The entire boarding house was quiet, which frankly he liked. No sooner had he shut his eyes but that he felt the telltale weight of slumber on his legs.

The steady thumping returned, annoying him. He was clearly hearing his own heartbeat.

Then he heard it again. A droning whine. The horrible groaning, echoing against the heavy clouds. The same sound he heard in San Francisco, rolling through the fog. Fading in the distance. The giant beast – the Prussian locomotive, built for the New Confederacy.

Turner flung off his blankets and raced back to the window. He had a reasonable view of the rail yard.

Nothing. No lights. No people. He stared hard into the night, hoping to catch the slightest movement, like a raptor waiting for the prey to show itself.

Nothing. Not even the thumping now.

A dream again? Instinct and experience said no.

Turner had donned his disguise of gentleman and entrepreneur, though the suit of clothes had seen some wear since he'd acquired them. Sherman had donned his disguise of Commanding General of the U.S. Army, which he insisted was indeed a disguise. If he was trying to hide his presence in Denver, his disguise was failing. Yet, Turner wondered, is he disguising the inner man who would rather be exploring the world with his wife? Or painting? Or sitting quietly in a theater box?

None of the other men would understand. They were focused on the marvelous engine idling on the track in front of them and trying to stand where neither mud nor snow had piled up.

"General, sir. This is the finest, greatest expression of technology you will ever find coming from the industrial might of these United States." The President of the Union American Locomotive Company of Cincinnati, Ohio, stood with his thumbs in his lapels and rocking on his heels, looking every bit the future politician. His men, all in heavy overcoats and woolen scarves, quietly applauded in the cold. The handful of Army men looked confused and stared at Sherman hoping to glean some direction. As Sherman clapped politely, the soldiers did as well.

The focus of the applause was a large, elegant locomotive with a new 0-4-4 wheel configuration, narrow smoke stack commensurate with coal burning for fuel, and wide cab with better visibility for the engineer and fireman. She hissed and popped as the boilers produced increasingly hotter volumes of steam, forcing the metal to expand in the winter air.

It was an elegant machine, painted in bright red, white, and blue – for the sake of presumed patriotism – with touches of gold on the lesser detailing. To Turner's mind, it was gaudy and likely to be nothing more than a photographic opportunity. He noted that the General was standing well back from the engine, outside of the camera's range. Sherman was not convinced and didn't want his name mistakenly associated with the new engine. These days, it did not pay to be misassociated with failed technology.

"Now, General, sir," the rail company's president said with swelling pride, "this marvel of modern machinery can reach seventy three miles per hour within four minutes from a dead stop. She burns two thirds the fuel of your average locomotive. All of this means, she travels further and faster than any other innovation on the rails."

Well, thought Turner; that could be very impressive. He glanced over at Sherman who remained politically attentive.

"And ... and! She is one hundred percent American. None of the nonsense from over the ocean."

"How so?" Sherman's face descended slowly toward a scowl.

"Why, sir, we have refused to employ electrical gadgetry and gimmickry that has failed the French and Germans with astonishing regularity. Even our British cousins refuse to adopt such designs that are based in the unstable business of electricity. All American, sir. We lead the world in politics and civilization, and now we will show the world how to conduct its use of technology. All eyes are on us, depending on us."

Sherman nodded but looked to Turner. His wife was always telling him not to bet his savings on what politicians and businessmen said of the Union's reputation abroad.

So went the rest of the morning, as they climbed around the magnificent vehicle. And for every word of posturing and assurance from the locomotive company, Turner's every silence suggested that there was more than was being said.

Carefully, Sherman maneuvered the pair of them into a more private situation, away from the company executives, journalists, and soldiers. "Alright, Turner. You saw that Confederate – Prussian engine back in San Francisco. Commander Willey's report said you described it to the last bolt, but since we never got our hands on it, I need you to give me a comparison."

Checking for eavesdroppers before speaking, Turner settled his body into a stance, which from a distance read as casual, and blew into his hands to warm them. "Sir. The Prussian-made locomotive, and I describe it as such since I doubt there was any Confederate design or even manufacture in it ..."

"They haven't the means?"

"Precisely. That machine is chemically fueled, reducing the amount one needs to carry. Cleaner too, sir." He held his hand up to cough, the smoky steam from the American engine was catching in his throat. "Depending on the chemicals, it would not billow out black smoke and leave a trail so thick and pungent that a twelve-year old could track it. When I examined that engine, there was no soot and no smell of burnt fuel."

"What else?"

"Only what I explained to Commander Willey. The Prussian engine is bigger by far, at least one and a half times as long, and quiet. Not silent – there's no design that could accomplish that, but quieter than anything I've ever been around. They employed electricity wherever possible. And while I've seen the European trains have difficulties with their electric engines, I do not agree that they are a failure overall. In my opinion, and please recall I've never claimed to be an engineer, the failure comes from not going far enough in employing electrical power into the design." For a moment, Turner winced, knowing full well he'd come close to speaking about Robur and the airship *Albatross*. "The engine has a streamlined appearance. Aerodynamic in shape which could give it speed despite its size. I counted the wheels, which were nearly as big as me. 4-8-8-4," he noted, hoping the General would understand the wheel configuration terminology. Four front and rear wheels, slightly smaller, then two sets of eight enormous wheels. "Rods the size of a tree. And a boiler of remarkable design – like nothing else out there."

Someone was staring at them. An old habit and skill, Turner knew when eyes were focused on him. "Sir, we are being watched."

Sherman pulled out a cigar box, offered one to Turner, who declined, and began lighting one for himself. It kept things looking average to anyone observing them. "Anything else?"

"It is dark. I don't mean that philosophically; I mean that it will be hard to see as compared to this …" he said, gesturing to the garish engine behind them. "And, regardless of its size or weight. It has been painted in black, with some roughness to its texture as to not reflect the light. No gloss to it." Crossing his arms and kicking slightly at the dirt, Turner looked around, hoping to catch sight of the person or persons observing them.

"They could hide it in a tunnel, or in a pass, and someone not looking specifically would miss it? That's how I'd use something like that." The General drew on his cigar for a moment. He was willing to wait. Turner needed to do what he knew best – find the enemy – it was an enemy. It could have been anyone watching them, but there was too much at risk to be careless. At last he looked up, directly at Turner. His hazel eyes were darker appearing – perhaps it was the light – or perhaps it was the sudden intensity behind them. "You haven't signed on; I respect your decision. But I can't trust anyone else right now."

"That is a shame."

"I need you to help me."

"Sir?"

"What I need is … a delivery of sorts … to someone who may already be in danger."

Turner frowned, distracted from his search of the area. "You need me to rescue someone? Have they started taking prisoners or …"

"Not yet, that I know of. Call it an assumption of future danger, how about that? He could be our top man in the field of electric power someday soon. He's young and used to working alone, like you, which means he's vulnerable - also like you. I need to deliver something very important to him. And to make sure he doesn't suddenly find himself in Prussia or Mexico. Or dead. I have special correspondences from …" A long pause was followed by a billow of smoke. "… a bunch of *old men*. I won't indulge my hope that you're rejoining us by trying to trap you or trick you into coming back. This is a one-time situation, perhaps one that's beneath your talents." He gestured with the cigar. "I'm operating outside of my usual sphere, and I must say it's uncomfortable. I suppose what I'm asking for is a personal favor, seeing as you might not be engaged elsewhere and I can't think of anyone else I can trust with it."

Turner was surprised that he didn't have to wrestle with the idea for very long. The Great Sherman trusted *him*? "Sir, I owe you to an extent I don't think you realize." He stared back at Sherman, looking for deceit in the General's eyes, expecting no such thing. Sherman was, however, eyeing Turner's scar showing slightly out of his collar. "I'll do this."

"Splendid."

"Who am I rescuing, or potentially rescuing?"

"You're heading south, Mr. Turner. Instructions will be waiting for you in Colorado City and Manitou Springs. Take a day at the spa – good for the health I hear. Splendid sightseeing. You'll deliver the package I'll give you tomorrow. " Sherman dropped the remains of his cigar into the dirt and crushed it into oblivion with his foot. "I'd send you off tonight but I must make a publicized appearance at a dinner. It was my excuse to be here, though I came to meet you and to get that correspondence into the right hands. Oh, and money. You'll need that too."

Turner nodded and quietly approved. He was broke. Not a single coin of his own rested in his pockets that could help him complete this task of Sherman's. "What am I not supposed to know?"

The General laughed a little. "Good question. You're not supposed to know that correspondence exists. I think you understand me. And, you're not supposed to know our man's around – no one is. We borrowed him a few months ago from France. Working for an American company out there. Damn brilliant – he thinks in ways you and I can only dream of."

"I've known men like that."

The General nodded, and strolled back toward the company men and soldiers milling about the pretty locomotive. He was starting to feel Turner's warranted paranoia. Nodding, he returned to the group of railroad men preening around their shiny engine.

Turner kept his hands in his pockets, attempting to appear unhurried. He didn't need to pretend he was cold. He calmly reviewed all he could see from his vantage point.

Waiting at the end of the platform, with a number of other well-dressed civilians gawking at the sublimely ridiculous locomotive, was a woman. Clad in black from head to toe, he decided she was in mourning. Tall, thin, striking in her simplicity. White skin showed on her chin, but the rest of her face was covered in a veil of sheer wool crepe. She was facing him squarely. He could feel her eyes on him, as if that were possible. In comparison to her pale skin her ruddy lips stood out, even through the veil and in the sliver that showed under the hem. She stood, unmoving, unemotional, watching. Her hands were gloved and clasped in front of her.

Behind her waited someone … something … in the shadows. Big. Broad. Undefined in detail. Masculine. Hovering just behind the woman in mourning.

Finally, she turned from him and inflicted the same intense glare on the locomotive and Sherman.

He had learned to trust that feeling of his skin crawling.

She had fallen asleep on her desk by the window, surrounded by a frenzy of chalked mathematical figures on blackboards. Some boards stood on proper frames, as one might expect to see in a classroom, yet others were propped up against the book cases, chaise, and tables. The parlor was a cluttered mess, which her friend recognized as a sign of trouble.

Miranda Gray knew her friend all too well. Chaos was a clear indication of anxiety. Lettie would leap into any mental exercise to avoid considering the details of an immediate problem. This day's problem was life threatening, and no amount of distracting equations would change that.

Lettie sat up with a start, momentarily dulled by the transition between dream and reality. Once she understood that she was at home and the figure in the room was Miranda, her heart rate lowered and she began to adjust her dignity.

"Did you solve the world's problem," Miranda said, dropping her muff and gloves onto the couch. The maid had not taken them at the door – Miss Gray was too frequent a guest for such formalities.

"None of them. I think I managed only to confuse myself more. The Prediction Model just isn't working."

"I thought you accurately predicted that Caribbean volcano?"

"But was wrong about the Andean eruption. My model is only accurate 50% of the time. Guessing could produce the same statistic." Slowly, Lettie began combing strands of black hair back into place. She'd become a bit thin in her person since the whole mess in the East Indies. After Krakatoa, she'd not been mindful of her health. And with the current threat against her life, she was fully distracted from eating. Worry was not her friend.

Miranda handed her the New College of London paper. "You were a smashing success at your lecture, or so they say. You're all over this edition."

"Good. I certainly paid them enough." She quickly moved papers and journals off the chaise so that Miranda could sit. "If I am to be believably visible doing what *they* think I should be doing, I certainly need good press."

"Was it my imagination or was that Doctor Watson who also attended?"

"It was."

"So, therefore, Mr. Holmes is still on the case?"

Lettie didn't bother to reply, she simply held out the letter she'd received from him.

"I've read it. *'Have looked into the details ... I am therefore unwilling to continue to explore your hypothesis until such time as more definitive data can be provided. I apologize for any inconvenience but I must decline further consideration. S.H.'* Sherlock Holmes, the man the papers adore and who has managed to imply that you are being a hysterical woman, worrying about nothing. I would use some vitriolic clichés but I have too much respect for myself. We don't need him. We can take on that Elegant Man on our own. I daresay take him on and win. I saw him, you know."

Lettie sat down ungracefully, having taken back the notice from Holmes. "At least Dr. Watson is still interested. But I can't help but feel that too many people are becoming involved; people who might get hurt."

"Let them try. I'm not afraid of them." Miranda sat up very straight. "Neither are you."

"Oh no, I am very much afraid."

For a brief moment, Miranda smiled at her friend. "You're afraid for that Yankee. You're concerned that you might be used as a hostage or might say something to get him hurt. I won't let you think another moment on that. People like this Elegant Man will do their worst simply because they can, not because you or I or that Mr. Turner have done anything at all."

"Quite reasonable." And Miranda was right, Lettie thought. None of this was her fault, though she'd been raised to take responsibility all the same. Oh why did society do that to women: make them at fault despite logical analysis? "Miranda dear – I don't want you thinking that I'm giving up, but – well, I am beginning to think that escaping violent eruptions, pyroclastic flows, and even that terrible man Robur have gone to my head. I think I can do anything, but I can't."

"This is no time for surrender. It's time to take the game and play it on another board with another set of rules."

Lettie couldn't help but smile. That was Miranda: never play the game by someone else's rules. "You have a plan?"

"Of course." Miranda unpinned her hat and set it down; a clear indication that she intended to stay for a while. "We'll need more game pieces on our side, new ones, if we are to save your Amour."

Her cheeks suddenly burned and she knew she was flushed. Amour? "Mr. Turner is not …"

All Miranda had to do was raise an eyebrow to quiet her friend. "Show me a woman who would go to all this trouble for a man she mildly thought well of. You sent Mr. Turner off with a kind letter and a great deal of potential for his future. For that, and for being associated with him against your will at first, you have been rewarded with a man threatening your life should you attempt to assist Mr. Turner further. That Elegant Man, as you've named him, followed you from the Indies to London and is spying on you! And yet, all you have to do is pretend Thomas Turner doesn't exist and all will be well. And yet … you won't. I think we both know why."

"I'm not wrong to think well of Mr. Turner."

"He kidnapped you," Miranda reminded her.

"I don't wish to discuss that," Lettie replied, half humorously. "It is no longer important. He made up for it. Did the right thing. Now it is my turn."

"It most certainly is." Miranda quietly revealed the handle of a small pistol lodged in her muff.

Lettie nodded, and patted her skirt pocket, which showed signs of stress caused by something mildly heavy. "I am not giving up."

Miranda raised her cup. "To *amour*?"

Lettie did not reply beyond a slight, coy grin.

Politics were of little or no use to him: nothing but lies and the liars that told them. Journalists were worse. They were beyond a bunch of simple hypocrites – they ruined lives.

If for no other reason than he couldn't stand to behave as a politician, Sherman hated being false with Turner. He liked the man. Every instinct told him Turner could be trusted – never mind all that nonsense of the past decade. While he also understood self doubt and self recrimination. And ... well frankly ... Turner had been a bit of a rogue, even if he had good reason to be.

That was the true reason he hated to have lied.

Ultimately, he might consider it a small lie, in comparison to the larger truth that they needed Turner *with* them and not *against* them.

Retired Admiral Porter was more than a little upset that an offer to return to the Navy was made to a man Porter thought was dishonored. He'd implied to Turner that Porter was happy to welcome him. In time, Sherman might be able to persuade Porter to relent.

He scribbled his fountain pen on a scrap of paper to get the flow going again, now that he'd refilled the ink chamber. Dinner had run late, as usual, and Sherman was used to filling the time with the stories and memories everyone had come to hear him tell. He always told them with a smile, though every part of his soul screamed that he should confess to being a flawed man and not worthy of their admiration. Lord, what he had done. The people who had died because of a single sentence from his mouth. All he ever wanted was order. How many people had been killed because of him?

The thought of sinking into the endless depths of depression he was known for scared him, it always scared him, and he pulled out a blank sheet of paper to write a soothing and calming letter home – now that his stressful duties had been done. Writing a letter to his wife would give him some peace of mind and a bit of distraction.

The letters from Grant, Porter, himself, two Congressmen, six prominent business tycoons, and Thomas Edison had been sealed in plain envelopes, marked only to Mr. N. T., and left without return addressing. These were tied together with the knot buried beneath a wax seal. It was a crude but effective way of ensuring that no one had tampered with the letters.

They were dangerous letters. Important men had to promise outrageous support and to sign their names in pledge to each other and to N. T. Methodologies were mapped out. Goals stated and confirmed. Strategies for foreign policy that circumvented the United States government. Someone might think they were treasonous. N. T. was to add his agreement and the whole delivered to a final safe location. The letters were protection for everyone who acquiesced to the scheme ... mostly from each other. The packet had seen some mileage, with the courier being chosen at the last possible moment. Were these to fall to any hostile parties, they would betray the existence of the *Old Men* and their intrigues, exposing their vulnerable new network, and potentially subjecting the Union to international censure. For a few of the men, it could mean economic ruin as their trust would be questioned. It would be a disaster. As far as anyone could tell, no one really knew about the Old Men. They had to remain secret ... working behind the scenes.

Promises were made. One letter guaranteed a laboratory anywhere the young N. T. wanted. Appropriate compensation, too. That alone wasn't damning. It was the request for whatever his mind could create that would serve to protect the country. Rumors were already circulating about lightning weapons and fuel efficient motors to put into military vehicles – even flying vehicles. History and those around him were already calling Sherman the creator of Modern Warfare, but what this young man had to offer would steal that title and change the world forever. The thought made Sherman feel queasy.

For his part, he would prefer the young man to be safe and out of the reach of foreign powers. That alone would suit him better, and his letter said so in a roundabout way.

Then there was his other lie to Turner, though he'd lied through omission. Today, the sailor might be able to escape uncomfortable questions. But sooner or later, he would have to provide the technical details of Robur's flying Clipper Ship.

Sherman's orders did not include asking … yet. No doubt about it, the questions would come. Surely Turner saw this?

Always subject to stress-induced asthma, Sherman set down his pen and walked over to the wash basin in the hopes of cooling his skin with the water, soothing his nerves.

The water felt good and drops clung to his beard. He looked up into the mirror and despised the man he saw. Indian killer? Traitor? Hero? Destroyer of Georgia? Or just a man doing what he had to, the best way he could? Bigot? Was he all of those things, some of them, or partially any one of them? More water. His chest was feeling tight. He pulled a towel over and began to dry his face. Joining with the Old Men was his last chance to make things right, freed from politics and the follies of public opinion. He would leave the country a more ordered place than he'd found it.

Looking again into the mirror, he found two extra pairs of eyes glaring at him. In an instant, a dirty hand clamped over his mouth and a Bowie knife came up under his chin. The towel fell to the floor.

"Amos, don't stand there. Git the letters. Anything he's written on, too." The drawl was distinctly indicative of Louisiana.

Amos tugged on the bill of an outdated, gray military cap and began seizing anything off of the desk he could find and shoving it into a canvas satchel. "Got 'em. Now, kill him and let's go."

"We ain't killin' 'im. Not if he don't give us no trouble. Not yet, at least. This here is Uncle Billy of Georgia fame." The knife wielder leaned in closer to Sherman's ear. "Ya hear that? You give me grief and I'll spill yer blood all over this hotel. Come quiet, an' I might let yer high self go. I might."

"Holy God Almighty," Amos tried not to cheer. "Hersh, we got ourselves General Sherman himself."

Sherman would have given anything at that moment to have been able to speak what was on his mind, but the situation kept him from making that fatal mistake. And he knew it. "Hersh" was not going to take much sass and the knife was already scratching at his skin. Little effort would be needed to cut his throat. For the moment, he cooperated. He needed those letters back.

Getting the great man to the door was easy, though awkward: Hersh was about four inches shorter than Sherman. Once into the hallway, the risk arose that someone might see them. They walked quickly down the carpeted corridor with Hersh still gripping Sherman by the mouth. The new electric lights were dimmed for the evening, leaving the hallway in an uncomfortably low illumination.

They approached the door to the staff staircase at the end of the hall. Amos strapped the satchel over one shoulder and across his chest, and pushed the door open.

The door slammed shut on Amos with such violence that it broke the man's nose and spilled him back into the hallway, howling in pain.

Turner flung the door wide open and stepped through, Colt in hand.

Hersh twisted until Sherman was forced to stand between them.

"Amos! Goddamn it boy, get up." But Amos was still writhing on the ground, clutching his nose. "Amos!"

"Let him be," Turner demanded. "You can walk out of here, just let him go."

Sherman shouted something indiscernible under Hersh's grip. Hersh tightened his hold and pushed the knife until it dented the skin. Any little struggle now would slash the skin open.

"I'll kill 'im, I'll kill 'im! Don't you come no closer!"

He was going to kill him anyway.

Turner flicked the gun – a small move that caught Hersh's attention.

Sherman got both hands locked onto Hersh's knife arm and pushed.

The knife lifted off his neck, just enough.

Turner fired nearly point blank.

Hersh dropped immediately and pulled Sherman along with him. The knife never did its work. The General shoved the arm away and crawled off the body, cussing under his shortened breath. Now his asthma was attacking his lungs. "Dispatches … in that bag." He pointed to Amos who was starting to get up, terrified at the sight of his dead partner.

Amos managed three steps through the door before Turner caught him by the shoulder strap and pulled him back.

Twisting, Amos slipped out from under the strap. He careened down the stairs, knocking over any staff who had arrived to see where the gunshots had been.

Sherman struggled a bit to sit up. "How did you know?"

"Old habit, sir. I can feel it when someone is watching. I waited to see if anyone followed you to the dinner and back here. This has been too easy."

Stopping to stare wide-eyed at Turner, Sherman muttered something about nothing being easy.

Clutching his bleeding nose, Amos ran out of the hotel, desperate to report back that Hersh had failed.

The *HMAS (Her Majesty's Air Ship) Prince Edward Albert* floated gently in the diminishing fog near St. James Palace. The airship's envelope was a garish red, white, and blue – the Union Jack –which disappeared beneath a blanket of fog every minute or so, only to emerge when the wind took a deeper breath. Beneath her was suspended a fine gondola of brass, glass, and multiple rotors for steering – which was somewhat comical for a simple passenger balloon. The turning screws actually had no real function except to make the airship look more up-to-the-mark than it really was. Flags of the countries which called themselves Great Britain snapped harshly and fluttered lightly in the changeable wind, often wrapping around the cables they were attached to. Those cables led straight down to the grass grove near the serpentine lane. It was more advertisement for the Empire than practical mode of transportation.

In the distance, the wind carried the sound of a brass band launching into a fast polka. Aromas of wet foliage, dirt, horses, and sausages drifted across the Row. The weather had not stopped any common folk from coming out to see the show. Some in the crowd that waited and watched commented loudly and pointed in the most vulgar way at the riders and horses that passed them.

Only the wealthy and well-known could afford to ride here, fulfilling the common man's insatiable curiosity. Most pretended their dignity was not at stake, but many had decided it wasn't worth thinking about and therefore there was no crowd at all – never mind the multitudes that showed up to watch the spectacle.

If one was very lucky, they might catch sight of some bloke's well kept mistress wearing the most sporty costume and haughty expression. Here a mistress could ride and display the gains from her labors fearlessly. No wife, also to be seen riding on the Row, would ever allow the rabble to witness her mortification at such a mistress's presence, thus an uncomfortable silence and détente existed between the legitimate and illegitimate partners.

And it was a fashionable thing to do in public. Miranda Gray had insisted she go. She'd been squeezed into the tiniest sized corset anyone could get her into, pinned into a heavy wool riding suit, and tossed up into a sidesaddle. Miranda had also insisted that she wear the dark green riding costume she'd recently purchased because it made Lettie's green eyes nearly glow with color. Miranda said it made her skin look warmer too – Lettie thought it made her skin look a tad olive. Well, at least the wool would help against the damp fog.

It had been a very long time since she'd ridden a horse but the basics were not forgotten. And truth be told, she was very comfortable riding aside and not astride. Part of her felt proper while another felt safer with her legs kept together closely under the flowing skirt. In her dreams she would never have thought it possible that she would be riding with the elegant fashion setters and rule makers. Any other day she would be elated.

Today, though, it was all forced.

"Wonder ooz darlin' that is?"

Lettie kept her gaze forward and recalled that Miranda had warned her that not everyone knew how to behave properly. Really, to suggest that every woman riding on the Row was someone's mistress was outrageous, but she was here for a better purpose and could ignore what didn't appeal to her mission. Miranda tried not to laugh from her seat on a lovely bay sauntering next to Lettie and her mare.

The fellow spoke louder still. "Wonder 'ow much she costs 'im per night?" The crowd around him burst into laughter, though a handful of women in linen aprons shushed him.

"Young man!" A fellow in all black, down to his shoes and stockings, lifted a scolding finger. His voice was moderately crackled, as too was his weather-worn face. His nose was long and bent slightly at the end, giving him the appearance of a malnourished hawk. The starched white neckband was all the relief he allowed himself in his dress, and by the rest of his description, he was an old fashioned reverend. "You should not be here, and certainly not watching this spectacle. Work, sir, have you no honest work? Idle hands. Idle hands. But if you must be here," his voice quivered with righteousness, "you need to recall your manners."

The young man was taken aback, as was Lettie who felt her sense of propriety slipping away. She needed to be seen, but not like this!

Miranda reached over and pulled lightly on the reins.

"Oh, please, let's not stop here," Lettie implored. She was certain a member of the New College faculty was here and would see her.

"We must, Lettie. That," and she politely pointed to a fellow in a crisp riding suit and outrageously tall hat, "is the commissioner in charge of all inspectors for the Metropolitan Police."

"Is it?"

"I think you need to meet him. But we had better keep up."

She didn't care that it wasn't done, Lettie looked over her shoulder, fearing that all the tailor's pins would burst out of her seams, and called down to the reverend, "Thank you sir."

"A pleasure! My dearest pleasure to assist." He seemed rather amused, indeed, he was quite puffed up.

Before she could speak again, Miranda had steered both their horses over toward a bend in the Row. "Let me catch up with him. Then we can make the introductions."

Sitting and waiting for Miranda to take such a risk was not what she had in mind when she'd confided in her old friend. Perhaps she should be more careful, she admonished herself. Speaking of scientific or exotic subjects was fine, but really, she may have made a mistake in drawing in anyone to her concerns. Gently, she tapped with her left heel and the crop in her right hand, urging her rather placid mount to amble over toward the trees. Fog was descending yet again and she could feel it on her face.

From her right, a pair of hands reached out from between two oaks and a large bush. She'd been surprised, and not prepared to keep her seat in the saddle. Falling. The first sensation was falling, then the fear that she would break her arm on landing. The fog was so thick she couldn't see the top of the trees from the ground.

No one could have seen what had happened.

A large hand grasped her by the jaw, and clamping down on her mouth, he dragged her backward.

The riding whip was still in her hands, she'd had that much sense. Lettie stomped down on the man's foot and twisted hard, out of his grip. Pins came loose and her jacket confined her less. She raised the crop to strike at the man who'd pulled her off her horse.

He had a friend.

An elegant friend.

"What, no hat pin this time, Miss Gantry?"

The Elegant Man stepped between Lettie and his man, Markus. The trip from the Indies to England had not softened Markus's constant appearance of offense and fury. But the Elegant Man looked quite worn himself. He produced a small caliber pistol and pointed it at her. "So very public, Miss Gantry. But you and I know that you are not a regular on the Row. I can only surmise that you are trying too hard to be seen. And that will have to stop."

"I've stayed in the public view because I don't want to be pestered by the likes of you."

"See how well it's worked. I've convinced my employer that he should meet with you. To see that I am correct in my assessment that you are a danger. But as you can imagine, he is not able to join us here, so you will come with me. We will require your acquiescence."

"I will not."

"This isn't a discussion."

"Has your employer failed to kill Mr. Turner? I told you he would. So you think that I will be a hostage? I think you mistake Mr. Turner entirely. I told you, there is nothing between …"

"Then why did you attempt to contact him?"

"I have not."

"Inquiries were made."

Damn you, Mr. Holmes, she thought without catching herself. First you said you'd be discreet, she recalled with growing frustration, then you said you weren't doing it at all. "Those inquiries were not made by me. I am not responsible for Mr. Turner having more acquaintances than me."

The Elegant Man stared, moderately put off. "Then I will confess that I don't know how you arranged it, but I know you did."

"Why are you so willing to take this risk – all to kill a man who had no interest in you or Pierre Hetzel or any of your nonsense?"

"I don't know how much you are aware of, though I will enjoy asking, but your Turner knows too much and cooperates too little. It is not a good combination. Now, as we have the advantage of the fog, you will come with me."

A fourth party joined them, by striding into the middle of it all and, with no warning, struck down Markus with a debilitating blow to the head. The Elegant Man turned to find a dapper man, with a moustache and a cane. Dr. Watson looked entirely unimpressed with the Elegant Man.

Neither moved. Which was a good thing.

First, a large book struck the Elegant Man from behind, then again across the jaw, then the stomach and finally the head again. It was remarkable that a little old Reverend could move so quickly, but the fellow with the cane seemed completely at ease simply watching the pummeling.

"Doctor Gantry, are you well?" The voice was annoyingly familiar, yet comfortable too.

Lettie squinted at the old Reverend; trying to see what she knew had to be true.

Slowly, the man took off his hat, to which a wig had been attached. Underneath was a full head of lightly oiled, brown hair. Away came the false nose and chin, leaving Sherlock Holmes grinning back at her.

"I hope you'll excuse the theatrics, Miss Gantry, but it seemed far more prudent for me to remain unattached to your case by all appearances." He began to chuckle to himself, very pleased with the work he'd done. Watson was less moved to enthusiasm but did look satisfied himself. "By the time I had made my first inquiry into the whereabouts of your Mr. Turner, I came to understand just how remarkable Hetzel's network was. And how wide ranging. I suspected that he would know all too soon that you had engaged my services and would send his agents to take action against you." He continued to remove his costume.

Lettie stared at him, waiting for the pounding in her chest to subside. The only thing she could hear was Holmes and a bird in the tree above her.

"Indeed, I must confess that I thought you were being a bit hysterical in seeing villains around every corner, but you were correct." The word rolled off his tongue with dramatic flair.

Lettie remained silent.

"I discovered the fellow over there," he pointed to Markus, "milling about your neighborhood. His superior here followed you around New College. One assumes that he would blend in better at the college, appearing as a business man while his comrade has the look of a tradesman who might be found in a residential area."

She stared at him.

"I am assuming you still wish to find Thomas Turner?" Holmes turned to her, half expecting the woman to be either swooning or crying. "You'll need to have a care, Miss Gantry. I cannot be expected to rescue you every time …"

Lettie moved to slap Holmes across the face, then wrapped her arms around him instead and kissed him on the cheek: none of which was proper for a lady, but under the circumstances, John Watson couldn't have approved more. Holmes made every gesture of being horrified yet resolved to her illogical, womanly behavior. Inside though, he was relieved that the plan had managed to go right … it could have gone so very, very wrong.

Contrary to what people assumed, the only good seats on an overland stage were just under the driver's seat, facing backward. All other riders were subject to a bone-rattling ride.

Actually, he couldn't quite fault himself for taking a stage from the railhead near Monument down to the burgeoning township at the base of the Pikes Peak. According to the schedule, they would be passing the remarkable geological features, quaintly called the Garden of the Gods, just before sunset. Even with a little give in timing, he should have made it to see the glorious red rocks. As the stage left eight hours late, he had to content himself with a partially moonlit view. Perhaps they could make it by sunrise. He'd just grown tired of train travel and this suited his need for a change, even if the three hour drive was on a dark and freezing night. The jostling of the vehicle down the road was terrible. Twice the stage had to stop to figure out where it was going. Wherever they might end up, they certainly weren't going to get there on time. It was going to be morning soon.

Odd that they didn't just put the passengers up overnight and leave in the morning? Well, the cost of the hotel came out of the driver's pocket, so perhaps he thought he could still make it at a civilized hour.

Turner sat facing forward sandwiched between tall foreign fellow who had not said more than two sentences and preacher who preferred to mutter to himself. At least he wasn't on the bench in the middle of the coach that was occupied by two brothers and a very large ranch hand – all facing forward from their eighteen inches of allotted space. The only female on the coach sat in the better location, riding backward, her seat kindly situated over the large, load bearing spring on the front axle. The remaining two passengers clearly had paid more for their tickets and were enjoying the ride much better than the rest. Today, no one but the two drivers was up top, but on a warm day, there might be as many as six additional men loaded onto the roof.

The foreigner folded his arms tightly across his chest, closed his eyes, and pushed himself into the corner. This gave Turner a bit more room and a chance to look out at the scenery. The coming sunrise was doing a fine job of lighting some of the way, reflecting off the snow and ice. Long grasses and shrubs were coated in sparkling white and bent together in the direction of the blowing wind. Fingers of ice stretched out from bushes and logs, frozen in place.

Now and then they would pass by a ravine between the mesas and few foothills, revealing the dappled mountains and the white head of Pike's Peak. Occasionally they passed a section of rock, worn away by the stream just below it: striations of brilliant color one could detect even in the darkness, topped with snow and decorated with icicles. A long tree, void of anything but the snow and frost replacing its leaves, stood out against the subdued landscape.

Turner's mind wandered as much a defense against the deafening rattle and jarring sway as any daydreaming might achieve. The prior night's events had only reinforced his expectation that he was headed back to his old life, like it or not.

He had been selfish and foolish. Sherman's letters had proven that point. Here were private correspondences whose very existence could cripple an industry, endanger individuals, and ruin reputations. Treason might even be suggested. What was it the general said: if it were up to him, he'd burn the whole packet? Sherman's idea was sound. And, despite the logic that physical evidence was too great a risk, the letters escaped destruction. No one trusted anyone. Proof. They wanted proof. So those dangerous letters remained intact, in Turner's coat pocket.

The good which came from the whole incident was small and unimportant to the great men, but remarkably significant for two people- Lettie Gantry and Tom Turner – it proved instructional for Turner. He knew what he had to do.

He leaned back against the damp leather seat. The coach had had no time to dry off from the poor weather and notoriously the stages were left out in the rain. The air was too cold and thin for it to have dried. Most of the passengers had dozed off from the boredom and constant rocking of the stage. A white billow of vaporized air spilled from his lips.

He'd finally done the right thing.

The words she'd written to him were read, re-read, and read again, until the contents of Lettie's letter were seared into his brain; memorized for the rest of his lifespan.

… In my science, I am happy. It is a lonely path on which I shall find many acquaintances and friends, few of whom I will dare to admit I will hold more closely to my heart than you. I shall not embarrass you by saying more on the matter as it is one which we will not be able to pursue. I shall only state that I will recall with great delight our conversations in Holland and aboard ship. I shall remember that evening before Krakatoa's last paroxysm quite dearly. I will regard you above others and think of you, knowing that you are following your heart far from me. If you can, regard me with fondness and remember me in kindness. I fear we shall not meet again, and in this, I am heartsick …

…Go find the Frontier before it is gone. Seek out the chance to change the world. Or live in the quiet peace, which you deserve. Know that I am as I should be, and will remain yours, in friendship and love,

Letticia

With that, in his room, waiting to walk to the stage offices, he burned the letter, envelope and all. He watched as the edges of the paper browned and curled, dissolving into a column of gray smoke and dirty ash. Stirring the bowl with the end of a pencil, the last of her handwriting disintegrated.

At first, he'd intended to empty the contents of the bowl into the wind blowing past his window. A melodramatic ritual he thought might free him at last from the dream he might ever know Lettie Gantry again. Something stopped him. An obsession he couldn't fight? An unquenchable hope?

The stage rocked violently, waking some of the folks. The tall man next to him seemed unperturbed. He glanced over at Turner and nodded. Reflexively, Turner checked on the letters and his leather pouch. Everything was where it should be. The packet of letters was large enough to fill and stretch his coat pocket, but that worked to his advantage making it difficult to remove them without his assistance. The pouch, purchased as a tourist trinket in Sacramento, hung on a cord around his neck, under his shirt, pressed against his chest – just where it had been all this time. The ashes of her letter had been carefully poured into a sheet of hotel stationary, with the header torn off, and folded into a tiny package that would retain the contents. That was how he could keep her letter and not put her life at risk should anyone see it. She was safe; certainly safe from his imprudent sentimentality. Damn it, he knew better.

"You are an easterner, I think." The tall man whispered with a genteel, charming expression. He was young, thin, neatly dressed. Dark curly hair was cut and oiled as a proper gentleman of fashionable taste would have it. Just beyond him, the sun was attempting to brighten the world and it gave Turner a much better look at the man. "Please excuse me, but it is your accent I heard when you assisted the lady into her seat."

Turner really hadn't thought about it, but to some ears he might indeed have a New England manner of speech, though he knew it was not so distinct as one from Boston or Portland. Navy life and travel had softened his pronunciations. The tall man, on the other hand, clearly had a strong of eastern European accent, perhaps Bohemian or Slavic? Another agent like Cairo, Turner considered?

"Yes, sir," Turner replied. "You are from Europe?"

"It is true, but I now reside here. I will become a citizen someday, I think. Are you an Army man? You have the look of a soldier."

That was an interesting observation. Turner had to wonder if this wasn't in fact another of Hetzel's agents. "No sir, I've never served in the Army," he answered quite truthfully.

For a time, the tall man seemed confused if not disappointed. "I had hoped to meet someone from the Army, as I have some questions," he said softly. The words seemed a bit awkward, as though he were asking something else.

"Thinking of joining?"

"No. I am not suited. But as I hope to remain in this country, I believe I should look for ways to be of use to it. I thought I might take up a correspondence ..." he said the word slowly, looking to see how Turner might respond.

"Correspondence seems to be the best way to start." Was this the man Sherman wanted him to meet? His instructions were waiting in Manitou Springs, but the General had also insisted he take *this* coach at *this* time. "While I'm no Army man, I can make some recommendations."

Both men stopped speaking, as though they understood each other completely and suddenly. Turner held up a finger, indicating that the tall man should wait for a moment. Meticulously, he looked to each passenger, to see who remained awake. The brothers in front of them were fussing over something they shared. The cowhand, lady, and wealthier passengers were asleep. The preacher was snoring a little.

"I am an acquaintance of a general and would be happy to introduce you to him."

"Precisely what I had hoped. I know one as well; who thought this unique but uncomfortable conveyance was essential to my visit to the West. And he recommends the spa."

"He does indeed. Probably thinks the spa is needed after this ride." Turner reached out, offering his hand. "Thomas Turner."

"Tesla. Nikola Tesla. Late of Gospić, Prague, Budapest and Paris."

N.T. There he was, just as Sherman had said. "A pleasure sir. I believe I can help you with that correspondence."

Tesla smiled very politely, but kept his hands under his arms. He seemed embarrassed, and yet reluctant to shake hands with Turner. As though making up for the slight, he leaned forward and replied, "How do you do? Yes. I hope you do not mind if I ask for that help once we reach Manitou. I believe such important things are best left in the hands of those who are better able to care for them."

Turner nodded. "I understand and would insist on the very thing." The man must not trust me, he thought watching Tesla's hands, or he just doesn't like touching people. He recalled that not everyone was as willing to be physical as many of his fellow Americans were.

Tesla smiled again, though not in a large toothy grin, which would have seemed foolish on him. "I must become a better judge of men. I mistook you for a soldier. You carry yourself in such a manner."

"Sailor." Turner said with an equal smile. "A sailor by former trade."

"An interesting direction you have now gone in," the scientist said, making Turner a bit nervous until he added, "you are now landlocked, are you not?"

"True, sir, very true. No ocean in sight sometimes makes a man like me jumpy."

"And you are not now?" He knew Turner would understand the question. Wasn't he just a bit concerned about unknown people, places, things, and the correspondence in Turner's pocket?

"I prefer to think of my experience as teaching me to be aware at times like this."

The road was long and lonely, which made Turner very, very nervous. It was his habit, though, to keep such thoughts from forming a concerned expression. No purpose in making the civilians anxious.

"You don't expect highwaymen, do you Turner?"

"No. I'm quite certain that hold-ups are far more frequent in dime novels than reality."

Someone pointed out the window, catching the attention of anyone awake. Due to flooding and ice patches, the coach had diverted into the Garden itself. It came to an abrupt stop, and after some cursing about taking another trail, the coach was maneuvered down through a wash out and up the other side.

"Good heavens," Tesla said pressing himself close to the window, attempting to avoid blocking Turner's view. "This place is well named."

As the coach rumbled along a less travelled road, a generous amount of sunlight hit the tops of the stone monuments. The orange reflected off the rocks and into the coach, bathing everything in red, until the road led downward and into a shaded ravine.

Jutting out of the ground, like pieces of broken glass, were enormous formations only Lettie could make sense of. Hogbacks, Turner had heard them called. Some were a white limestone, pink in the morning glow, all lined up running north to south. Next to them, often touching were the great red sandstone rocks uplifted vertically to form a barrier to those in the interior of the Garden. With hogbacks of various colors and gigantic sizes on both sides of the road, the rising sun was soon cut out completely.

The stage drew up sharply again. This time the driver and the shotgun messenger were hotly debating the presence of a tree log in the middle of the trail.

Gunfire.

Nothing was so distinct in its shocking noise as gunfire.

What was being shouted over the clamor of men running toward the vehicle and horses reacting to the chaos was indistinct. The intention of the shouting was entirely clear.

The stage had halted so quickly that everyone inside was awakened and set on edge. Things moved fast. Both doors to the coach were pulled open by men who hid their faces under bandanas. Whatever their intent in hiding their faces, they had not considered what telltale signs identifying them still remained. Old Gray uniforms, older model guns, a certain twang to their speech, worn saddles, tools needed to herd cattle … all of it gave away some clue that Turner silently took in. As Tesla opened his mouth, no doubt to comment on Turner's earlier assurance that robbers only committed such crimes in novels, Turner shook his head and with the slightest gesture waved him off.

One by one, the passengers were forced to leave the coach. The driver and the shotgun messenger were forced to stand by at the left-hand side of the vehicle. The preacher muttered an all purpose curse at the thieves, which fell on deaf ears. The lady fared a bit better than the others, in that she was allowed to keep her watch and wedding ring. Everyone else was stripped of any valuables with alarming efficiency and sent scurrying into the Garden with the guarantee they wouldn't be killed if only they ran without looking back.

Tesla was pulled out to the left, Turner to the right. Last ones.

The scientist was quite literally chewing on his lip to resist reacting to being touched. He hadn't a great deal of cash on him, but his watch was fine as were his hat and his gloves. It was a wonder they didn't take his clothing, most certainly his wool overcoat. Unlike the other passengers, the thieves were not so quick to send him off into the wilderness and made him stand with his hands held up, next to the driver.

At that moment, Turner was prodded behind the coach and could see what he feared. The money, the jewelry or watches, they were only minor spoils. Two men were going through Tesla's pockets with some focused determination. Another two men climbed onto the coach and began throwing luggage out of the canvas boot at the rear. They were looking for something quite specific.

One advantage to being broke was that Turner *looked* broke, in a gentleman's sort of way. He had nothing worth stealing at first glance.

"What's fillin' up his pocket?" A man from up top on the coach called down.

Before Turner could say anything, another fellow replied, "the Letters. That's him, from the hotel."

Turner faced the man behind him who was pointing excitedly at his full coat pocket. Pulling off his bandana, the man walked up to Turner to make certain he could see his face, broken nose and all. The fellow from the attempt on Sherman's life: Amos. Both eyes were blackened as often happened when one had their nose smashed in by a door. "He killed Hersh."

Several guns were pointed in Turner's direction as Amos dug the letters out of his coat.

Amos held them up. "I got 'em!"

It was to the scientist's advantage that no one really worried about him. Tall but too thin. Very proper looking. Almost a touch effeminate by American standards. Tesla was unexpectedly quick. A rectangular box with a handle became his immediate weapon on choice and he wielded it with logical swiftness. Of the men searching his pockets prior to that moment, the young scientist struck the first with tremendous force. The driver was quick to jump into the fray and had another fellow pinned to the ground.

Turner seized Amos by the collar and slammed his face into the coach, likely breaking his nose a second time. It took a brief wrestling match with Amos to get the letters but he succeeded.

The shotgun messenger was the fastest amongst the group and took up a dropped gun, fired at the two men on the roof, killing one and prompting the other to jump off. The last robber ran into the trees, shouting for reinforcements, happy to avoid what was becoming a fire fight.

"Everyone out of sight!" the driver screamed, plucking a pistol from the prone body of the thief in front of him. "Get away from here!"

Turner easily took the revolver from Amos, who lay curled up into a ball, holding his nose again. Once he was closer to Tesla, he pulled the scientist in close, handed him the letters, and whispered sternly, "You have to get out of this, sir. No matter what. Now follow me."

"No, I must ..." Tesla turned toward the pile of luggage.

"I'll get whatever it is. We have to go now!"

He and Tesla darted into the sharp and cutting branches of the low shrubs, not stopping to look behind them. He shoved past the branches of some sort of tree, dropping snow and needles down onto his own head. They had to get into the rocks. Trees and bare bushes were neither good to hide behind nor able to offer protection from bullets.

"Spread out. Find 'em," was all anyone said or needed to hear. There was no telling how many reinforcements were now out there looking for them. A few distant shots belied to Turner that the driver and shotgun were headed away from them. He silently wished them luck.

"I want that son of a bitch!" Amos cried out.

After a moment, Turner was sorry he hadn't looked behind him more frequently.

Tesla wasn't behind him. Damn it!

Circling back, Turner climbed out of the bushes to find the scientist locking a very large piece of luggage with a key. As the man's pocket was not bulging from the letters, Turner guessed that Tesla had put them into the case. The scientist was taking a terrible chance.

Tesla never looked up. "Mr. Turner. We must hide this – it contains more that you can imagine. It is more important than my life or the letters, do you understand?"

"One of your inventions?"

"Yes. A very powerful one. And it must not be taken by anyone." As Tesla stood up, tall and thin, worried and frightened by the possibilities, he revealed to Turner a strange looking gun that must have been kept in the luggage. There was no cylinder or hammer, which suggested that the weapon did not carry bullets. Shiny but not glossy, it almost looked like a child's tin gun.

From the south, the voices remained at a whisper which the rocks turned into a boisterous conversation, until one of the party heard the echo's effect and shushed everyone.

The scientist found himself being grasped by the collar of his overcoat and dragged away from the pile of passenger luggage. He allowed Turner to pull him along to a spot behind a row of thick bushes and substantial boulders, his eyes never leaving his bag. No one could get their hands on that!

"Mister Nikola Tesla?" The voice called out with an accent that was neither British nor German, but something distinctly European. In fact, it was relatively close to Tesla's speech patterns, which by the look on Tesla's face annoyed him. "Mister Thomas Turner, as well, I see. This is rather efficacious, don't you think?"

Turner said nothing at all but stared at the little man in wire-rimmed glasses being followed by a large group of men in cowhand gear and tossed-off old Confederate uniforms. Beside them were the men who'd robbed the stage. The wide hat some had on their heads appeared the same, with each brim creased or bent differently. Each man wore heavy canvas trousers, and gun belts, with a variety of weaponry held in place by them. They were a contrast to the Egyptian, whose size and fussiness set him almost comically apart almost.

"Oh I do hope we *are* disturbing you. You see, it would be a terrible thing to miss out on meeting you, Mister Tesla. I am certain that your new weapon, which I have heard of, will be very successful, but I must be completely honest when I tell a buyer that I have seen it work for myself. I hope you will oblige us with a test. If you will come with us now … you and Mr. Turner … I'm sure we can provide you with a better recompense than the poor American Army."

Tesla looked at the Egyptian as though he were made of dirt and something unspeakably malodorous. "*I am content amongst the rocks,*" he said in a language Turner had not heard before. "*I see no need to be cooperative with a common thief.*"

"*How very rude,*" Cairo replied. "*You have been spending too much time with Mr. Turner and living in this barbaric country. You must come with me now.*"

Turner recognized his name but otherwise, nothing.

"*I will say it again,*" Tesla replied in the same language. "*No. I have no interest in …*" Realizing that Turner had no idea what was being

51

said, he quickly translated: "This person is not understanding that I am not interested in working with him or showing him any of my developments. Apparently, he is also from Budapest, or at the least knows the language."

"Will you not formally introduce us, Mister Turner?" Cairo called over.

Turner's eyes narrowed. "Didn't I throw you off a train?"

Tesla was mildly amused.

"I have decided for now to forgive you for that. Holding a grudge can be helpful in business but not very often, therefore I am choosing not to. Is that not advantageous to you and me?" Cairo smiled in a bizarre way that made Turner's skin tingle slightly. He folded his hands, showing he had no intention of doing anything physical; such things were to be done by the men waiting for his signal.

Tesla whispered, "You threw that man off a train?"

"He was trying to kidnap me at gun point and threatened to shoot civilians if I didn't go quietly. I acted on a third option."

"How very rude." Tesla thought for a second. "I mean his attempted kidnapping."

Turner's lopsided smile started to fade as quickly as he'd made it. "Mr. Cairo, what makes you think that you can just invite us and we'll go?"

"Because, Mister Turner, I have brought many well armed men to enforce my invitation. And I believe that neither you nor Mister Tesla desire to be shot, is that not so? Perhaps there is more that we can arrange for – a bargain perhaps?"

Shaking his head, Turner said out loud what he was thinking, "I have no idea what he would trade. I am certain he is lying."

The Egyptian was becoming agitated. "I think that we will take your notebooks and invention, Mr. Tesla, in any case."

Tesla turned toward his luggage, piled up with the other bags off the stage. The large case; bigger than any other box or case. Such a beautiful thing it contained. Elegant. Efficient. And, there were the letters. A pair of the Egyptian's men were beginning to open it. "Mr. Turner, there is something I must do ... I have to expend a charge. It may drain the pistol, but, I cannot allow that bag to fall into their hands."

"Agreed. That's an electric gun?" He stared at the large case, remembered the letters … why couldn't things be easy? There wasn't another answer he could give Tesla. The bag contained too much that the Prussians or New Confederates could use against the Union; it had to be destroyed. He nodded and realized that this might change his tactic entirely.

Tesla leveled the electrical pistol at it and fired. At first, nothing happened. Then the gun itself began to glow in blue and white. An arc, like a lightning bolt, flashed out of the muzzle and struck the bag which flew into the air and obliterated itself, along with several other pieces of luggage. Whether it was his proximity to the electric explosion or the idea that he'd just destroyed a work of art he'd created, Tesla felt physically wounded. His ears were instantly assaulted by the huge crack of thunder the arc generated.

Cairo and the cowhands either dropped to the ground or ran in different directions as the explosion subsided and the fire spread to the remaining luggage.

It was Turner who was surprised that the suitcase had exploded into molten bits, and he seized up Tesla to get him as far away as possible. They'd retrench further back in the rocks, now that any movement was covered by the panic and confusion below.

"It was beautiful," Tesla moaned.

"The lightning? Yes, it was. Can that gun fire another shot?"

"No. The means to charge it was in there." Tesla gestured disheartedly.

It seemed that the small agent could howl like a coyote, as he ran to where Tesla's machine had been. A number of Hungarian words were screeched in fury.

"Such language!" Tesla almost turned to go back. How dare anyone say such obscenities toward his creation? How dare anyone speak of the dead in such a way?

"We need to keep moving, sir. You are the one who must survive this. You can make another." The ground was getting softer in parts and running was all the more difficult. "You don't have any other weapon?"

"No," Tesla said sheepishly, reaching out to pull himself up an outcropping, his French shoes slipping on the sandy rock. "But I may have some small charge left. Enough to scramble a man's senses."

The cracks in the giant rocks were large enough to fit an arm or a whole person into. Some had small caves worn at their base. The white rock was almost peeling off of the darker red sandstone rock. Turner stared up toward the top of the behemoth they rested near. It blocked much of the sky from view. He crouched down next to Tesla who was catching his breath. The Hungarian scientist was not lazy or ill-exercised, but Turner felt it too – the altitude of the area sported thin air. Neither Turner nor Tesla had grown accustomed to the elevation. Heaven help them if they had to escape into the mountains.

"Please excuse me, Mr. Turner." Tesla whispered, gulping up as much air as he could. "The laboratories in New York and Paris do not prepare one's lungs for this sort of exercise. I will be ready in just a moment. I hope we have the time?"

Turner only nodded.

"How many bullets do you have left, Mr. Turner?"

"Two. That'll hardly do the job."

"We have mine." He held up the weapon. "I'm sure of it: one weak shot. But it may do the damage of several bullets."

Overhead, the sun climbed into the sky, adding little to no more warmth. They moved quickly to the sunnier side of the hogback and settled down. Waiting was the hardest part for both men. They listened, reacting to every little noise. In the morning air and somewhat empty environment, every noise should have been directly attributable to the stage robbers. Should have.

"The letters are gone. Gone with my invention. You do understand that?" Tesla almost sounded relieved and yet … "They were an agreement between men. I should not like to enter this venture without certain guarantees."

For a moment, Turner was tempted to question such a brilliant man about his clear naiveté. Yet Tesla was young and experienced only in the semi-monastic life of an academic. Very much as Lettie had been. "Mr. Tesla, I understand your concern, and believe me, more promises have been told as lies than I can count. Sometimes," the words were pinched; forced so that he could hear them for himself too, as they had as much weight on his life as on Tesla's. "Sometimes you have to take the chance and believe in what you're doing." Why was he arguing on the behalf of the Old Men? Because they were his heroes. He had to. "I can't speak for every man who wrote one of those letters, only those men I've known by reputation. I owe one man my life and will always feel the obligation. You saw the letters, they existed in truth. They were signed and sealed at great risk."

Telsa agreed, with an odd look on his face, as though one of his experiments had provided an unexpected outcome. "That is true. And I would have added my own set of promises to the collection. Edison promised me a bonus. Well ... " His voice faded a little, as if knowing the lack of written proof was going to be a problem later. "You know that I am not even officially here? They brought me over early, these Old Men of yours. I will officially arrive in the country next year."

"I'm asking you to trust those men. To trust that you decided to join them for a reason. Something had to have convinced you this wasn't an act of madness."

"It is always an act of madness." Tesla looked back out toward the Garden. "Yes. Though I am less inclined to dismiss it as a gut feeling." He adjusted the sight on his electric pistol. "You do not strike me as a man prone to trust. Why have you, as they say, signed on with them?"

Turner felt something hollow in his chest. "I've only been asked to do this one thing."

"Just this? One does not need to be jaded by the weary world to know that you are not meant for this one assignment alone. You have done this sort of thing before, and will again."

"An intelligencer's life."

"A hero's. You are doing this with no promises ... no letters. What does it say about me that I require guarantees? No, Mr. Turner, the man who saves another or serves a greater purpose is the man one should aspire to be like – even if he is quiet about it all and embarrassed by the truth of it – as you are now." Before the Yankee could protest the compliment, which Tesla knew he would, he continued. "I think, Thomas Turner, I shall follow your lead and not worry about letters and handshakes and promises. But I do have one doubt."

"And that is?" Turner replied, grateful the compliments were ending, since he didn't know what to do with them anyway.

"If these men do not see you for what you are and have not made you an offer to join with them, I doubt their wisdom. Ah ... no

... they did offer you a position, didn't they? I am a scientist. It is obvious through observation that this venture has too many hopes and goals for the greater safety of the nation to be designed by foolish men. Am I right?"

"Yes, sir."

"Then I will extract a promise from you. I will join without letters or promises, and I will do whatever it takes to properly participate – I was quite truthful when I said I will become a citizen one day – if you will agree to join this venture. What do you say?"

Turner must have stared at the scientist for a long time. "Mr. Tesla, it's more complicated than ..."

Wheels, creaking joints, horse hooves – all distinctive sounds of a wagon pulling in behind them.

Tesla was signaled by a silent gesture from Turner to stay low to the ground. Carefully, Turner positioned himself to look at what was approaching. They were trapped between forces if these were Cairo's men.

Turner hadn't heard the wagon approaching over the noise of Cairo's screeching in the distance and Tesla's extraordinary offer. It didn't seem to be in a tremendous rush but it was moving quickly enough. Keeping low to the ground, he crawled over to where he could look down on the sound, fully anticipating around five robbers. On the sunnier side of the rocks, one man in a travelling suit seemed to be searching for something, perhaps them? Turner waved Tesla over to look.

"I know this man," Tesla replied with relief.

"You sure?"

"My associate, Batch."

"We may have to take a chance, Mr. Tesla." Turner stood up and waved.

Batch was surprised and somehow pleased to see anyone, but noted the gun in Turner's hand. Before the obvious misunderstanding could arise, Tesla joined Turner. After indicating his own weapon, Tesla signaled his friend to be quiet and to stay low.

Batch was rather spry, scampering up the hill to where the two men were awaiting him. He was almost excited to be there and, no sooner had he arrived, but that he began asking questions. An Englishman, by the sound of it, and a businessman.

Turner silenced him with a polite gesture. "Sir, do *you* have any weapons beyond that rifle?"

Batch smiled. "Just this," he said, brandishing his nice, new, hunting weapon. Looking at Turner and his revolver, he energetically asked, "Can you draw that quickly, like they describe in the newspapers? This is all terribly thrilling, you know?"

Nearly exasperated by the ridiculous enthusiasm, Turner rounded a bit harshly on the newcomer, who pushed his way past them to peer out into the garden, hoping to catch a glimpse of the robbed coach.

"Mr. Batch, what are you doing here?"

"Helping your escape, clearly."

"No sir, why are you here. How did you know to find us?"

"Ah well." Batch sat down rather disappointedly having not seen very much at all. "You see, your stage is late ... very late. And while the last station wired down to us that you had left from Monument, you simply hadn't arrived in reasonable time. So, I came out to look for Nicky here."

Tesla's face scrunched up at the nickname, but otherwise he was glad to have his friend.

"How are the roads in and out of here, Mr. Batch?"

"Dreadful. We'll never be able to 'make a run for it' as you western men say. Ice, mud ... slow going."

Sharp voices called out to one another, causing all three men to press themselves into the mud even deeper, to avoid being seen. Cairo's men were getting closer, and Turner knew that there were too many limits to the fighting skills of the men he was with. Besides, Tesla needed to go south to Colorado City.

Turner looked down at his hands for a long time, occasionally twisting the Colt in his fingers.

Tesla had a bad feeling. "What can we do? There will be enough light out there for them to find us easily, and if we cannot escape quickly ..."

The key was the silly but well-meaning man who'd arrived at the best time. Turner decided he had a greater respect for Tesla's friend. "Mr. Batch, I can hold them here, but you need to get Mr. Tesla to the Army now. He needs to be in protective custody. There's a post in Colorado City and another near Manitou Springs."

"What of you, sir? It's entirely intolerable to leave you here alone."

Turner smiled and looked back at the Englishman. The fellow was entirely serious. "Mr. Batch, my job is to see to it that you don't become prisoners of the Prussians, the Spanish, the Confederates, or whomever it is out there that General Sherman thinks might want to hold you. It would seem best that I keep them busy, long enough for you to get Mr. Tesla to safety."

Tesla straightened up. "I am quite willing to defend myself ..."

"Yes sir, I know that. But it's a risk you cannot take. For the sake of what you may do with your intelligence, and the letters you now represent, you need to stay alive and free. If I can do nothing more, I will do this to help you escape."

"Well … I don't know what to say …"

Turner waved off any further comments. "They didn't come here prepared to fight this hard. That's to my advantage. What we're seeing is all we're getting, as the saying goes." He pointed toward the Egyptian and the remaining men in the distance, or at least where he thought they were. "Walk the horses out and be as quiet as you can. Stay to shadows whenever possible. And don't look back."

Tesla held his electric pistol out for Turner. "One weak shot left."

"Tempting. But I had better not."

Batch spoke up and shoved his rifle at Turner. "Then you'll take mine. Daresay we'll make do with the fancy thing Nicky here made. Got a box here with a few more cartridges in it. That should give you some fire-power." Batch held out his hand for Turner to shake. "Good luck, old boy. We'll make for Colorado City. More people are there and, as you say, a bigger Army presence. And, perhaps a few extra places to hide if we must." Now there was some bright thinking.

Turner narrowed his eyes to see out into the remaining dark, where Cairo and his men still hid. Sunlight in the whole Garden would not be long – places to conceal himself in the shadows would start diminishing. "Mr. Batch, I approve of your plan. Please take nothing for granted or anyone at their word. And if it isn't too much trouble …"

"Yes?"

"Let the army know what happened."

Batch looked confused but Tesla understood. "We will send someone back. There are a handful of civilians in need of assistance out here too." With some reticence, Tesla offered his hand. "I … I usually do not … shake …"

"Thank you." As they shook hands, Turner had a feeling that the young inventor was far more than deeply ashamed he would escape where Turner would not. He wasn't a fighter; that much was true. This semi-failure had always been a possibility.

"Mr. Tesla, I look forward to meeting up with you in Colorado City." What a lie, but he could let Tesla go without hope that he could regain some bruised honor in sending a rescue party.

"You will remember your promise to me, yes?"

"I never made a promise." His voice belied his humor.

Tesla shook his head. "Your protest only confirms your promise. If not to me, then to yourself, Mr. Turner. You are greatly needed. The world is full of men who need assurances; it needs more like you who will travel the distance with neither a passenger ticket nor luggage, only a destination." The metaphor sounded appropriate. "We will send the Army back for you."

Turner was certain he wasn't going to be rescued. But the other passengers would need help and there the Army would likely be successful.

The cold was brutal.

He warmed his hands and waved confidently at the two men who climbed down the side of the ridge and took the wagon and horses slowly, quietly, carefully away.

Sometimes he caught himself holding his breath and having to purposely take a deep draw of air into his lungs to keep from becoming dizzy.

He could see Batch and Tesla beyond the edge of the Garden. No one behind them.

But that wouldn't last if anyone thought to chase them. Cairo and the robbers needed to be distracted.

A slight movement to his right. He aimed carefully. It moved again. A garish bandana and wide brimmed hat. Turner took the shot, slid down behind his rocks, and shifted his position over to the far left. His shot was met with a series of miscalculated bullets striking at his old spot.

He could keep this up until he was out of ammunition. But, without ammo, he couldn't keep them back – they'd find him. That too was an advantage. He'd done this before, allowing an inevitable capture, on his own terms.

The cold was truly brutal.

After an hour, even with the sun shining down on him, it was too cold. And he was out of bullets.

Things were likely about to get colder.

Cairo was happy, but many of the men with him who had even the slightest experience knew there was something very wrong with Turner's sudden appearance. He walked into the middle of their group, just like that, hands up. After leading them around the Garden, over rocks and through bushes, always with an enticing noise, a well-aimed shot, he just walked up to them.

Amos had to be sent off before he made too much of a scene, which was saying a great deal compared to Cairo's overreactions.

After long minutes used up in searching Turner, getting half answers, and realizing that he was very much alone, it was becoming clear to the dimmest among them that Turner was keeping them occupied.

"Where is the scientist?" The Egyptian kept looking, becoming more panicked with each second. None of the three remaining cowhands could answer. One kept his grip on Turner. "You are very aggravating, Mister Turner. Don't you think I can catch him?"

"No, actually, I don't. I think he's half way to Denver by now. Or better, boarding the train up north at Monument for Fort Laramie, where the Army will look after him. You've spent quite a while chasing me around here. What, two – three hours?"

Cairo kept looking like he might start weeping at the sight of the mound of melted metal and burnt leather that had been Tesla's baggage, and likely something quite valuable. "This was a perfectly good invention I'm sure and you destroyed it."

"If you wish to be correct, the scientist destroyed it. And since he built it, it seems only fair that he should do with it as he liked. Apparently he didn't like you stealing it."

The Egyptian sneered at the mess for a moment then addressed the lanky, unbathed man next to him, covering his mouth so that he wouldn't have to smell him. "Did you find anything?"

"No. No letters, no more weapons, nothin'."

Turner's lopsided grin showed up. "Empty handed? I don't think your employer ... or is it now employers ... will appreciate you showing them empty hands."

For a moment, the Egyptian stared silently at the ground. Then, he aimed his anger toward Turner. "I have been very patient with you, Mister Turner. Very patient. But you have no right to stand there, smug, making inconsiderate comments. It's a bad habit you Americans have. It is very cruel of you to behave like this. It is very clear that you do not know how elegant this business is; you are just another uncouth Yankee destroying anything you can't have. You are sure you know everything and do nothing wrong. I can assure you that you are mistaken, especially now." Sadly, he glanced back at the molten debris. "It might have been so lovely. You should be ashamed. I'll bet it was a weapon, and a beautiful one at that."

"I've seen the effects of war, Mr. Cairo, and modernized weapons. There is nothing beautiful about it."

"You shouldn't have done it," he whined. "Maybe my employer will want to destroy something in return. Something you believe is beautiful? Then you'll know what this feels like."

What the hell did he mean by that?

Lettie? No, Hetzel had no reason to harm her. The letters might have been an interesting trophy in his intelligence collection, but not something he'd risk the attention harming Lettie in England might cause. No. It couldn't be what Cairo meant. Then again, what if the employer was, as Turner had suggested, the Prussians or the New Confederacy? Yet they didn't know about Lettie, except perhaps, through Cairo. His stomach felt hollow.

In the distance, a train blew its steam. It howled against the rocks and almost seemed to cry out in pain and anger. Turner listened. He knew that sound. He'd heard it in San Francisco, where the fog made it eerie and threatening. People had thought it a dreadful spirit come to drag away the less righteous to some hell of their own making. It caused grown men to lock their doors and windows in fear. And it was fearful.

Trains? Threats? Things were getting out of hand. "Now just a minute ... I'm getting tired of you using people ..."

"I believe we may go now, not empty handed though. Perhaps we may yet learn something of value from you Mr. Turner."

Cairo blotted his forehead for a moment. "I think you will tell us many things."

Her footsteps caused a slight crunching of the snow and gravel, otherwise she made no sound. Cairo was instantly aware of the woman walking up to the gathered men and prisoner. Black clothing. A hidden face with only lips and chin showing. Her bleak attire was supplemented by a fur wrap for the cold, but nothing else was different about her since Turner had seen her in Denver.

She said nothing.

Had he not heard her footsteps he would have thought she was a ghost, following him.

Without looking to his captive, for Cairo was now attentive to the presence of the woman, he ordered one of the cowhands, "Please render Mister Turner available to travel with us. The rest of you, ride north to … ah, Monument. Find the scientist."

Someone amongst the cowhands understood Cairo without discussion.

A blow to the back of his head was all it took to reduce Turner to a pile of human flesh on the ground. It was a dangerous option – for Turner. Not every man so pistol-whipped would regain consciousness. And by the unimpressed expression on Cairo's face as he glared down at Turner's unmoving body, he hardly cared if Turner ever moved again.

The monstrous locomotive was not labeled with a charming, nostalgic moniker as had been the dirigible, *Albermarle II*. There was no desire to link the frightening machine with the past or a specific cause. The beast did not inspire such sentimentality. What it did inspire was a dumbstruck awe at its size and an immediate comprehension that even the most impressive claims would fall short of the reality. Turner had told Sherman the engine was huge, but now, facing it as he was, he realized just how grotesquely underestimating he'd been. Had his memory failed him or was it that that locomotive was now in a different environment? In the open. With two freight and two passenger boxes attached.

The boiler was in design a great, long cylinder, yet with so many pipes and lines protruding from it, the shape was indistinct. Inside this body had to be a pair of Wimshurst generators, or electrical power creation of some sort. The headlamp, like the eye of a Cyclops, glowed in a chemical orange, dimmed as to not blind the workers.

As if in response to his stare, the locomotive spit hot water droplets all over the ground at his feet, along with grime and grease. Crewmen raced to get their work done, wary of the occasional steam blows that created fog around it, giving the engine a ghostlike appearance. It did not reflect the early morning light which left an impression that it wasn't really there. Creosote soaked rail ties filled the air with a sickening, pungent smell, mixed with oil and overheated metal... and the strange liquid fuel they utilized in place of coal. He'd seen their boiler and fuel box back in the San Francisco warehouse. With the pain in the back of his head still throbbing, the whole scene made his stomach turn.

Twice he thought he might ask about Cairo's threat. Two cowhands had a brutal grasp on his arms, propping him up and occasionally dragging him along as the effects of being knocked unconscious lessened.

The monster softly hissed: a snake confidently waiting to strike.

The Egyptian left his prisoner there, facing the locomotive, to contemplate the machine's size and worth. It would put Turner in the proper state of mind, he was certain. "I think, Mr. Turner, you will tell me everything I wish to know. You and I both know that you would rather not have dealings with my esteemed employer. I will tell you that he has plans to incorporate you and your talents into his improved legions. And this," he added smiling in the strangest fashion, "is so abhorrent to you and me that I believe you would choose death instead." Cairo blotted his forehead with a linen handkerchief. Taking his time was pleasing him to no end, though he had to suffer the mountain weather the whole while. Yet, Turner had to be making the comparison of the engine with the mechanical enhancements that Hetzel's army had jutting out of all sorts of physical places: arms, legs, heads. The comparison would only help Cairo. "Mr. Turner, I confess that I admire you, despite everything. You are not just a lucky man, you are clever and resourceful. I have to wonder if some of your luck rubbed off on me. It was too bad, though, that we did not obtain the correspondence your General was so protective of. A shame."

"Mr. Cairo, you have a penchant for exceedingly long explanations, but today I think you might want to just get to the point." Turner kept looking at the great iron pilot, the "cowcatcher," at the front of the train and the two platforms built over the pony truck -front wheels and the body-sized cylinder boxes. Water dripped from the radiator onto the track.

The Egyptian put away his handkerchief, moderately amused. "How American. Yes, I suppose I do talk too much, but I find I cannot situate myself with conversants quite as informed as I prefer, thus I always have to explain things. Despite our difficult relationship, Mr. Turner, I have enjoyed our conversations." He frowned for a moment and recalled Turner's fist ending the first such conversation. No matter, he could forget that if desired. "To the point then. I would be just as happy to let you live as to kill you here and now."

"I thought those were your instructions from Hetzel."

"Monsieur Hetzel is a leaf in the wind, changing as the season requires. Yesterday, he wished an alliance with you. Today," and

Cairo was enjoying his embellishments to the truth, "he wishes to have you *improved. Enhanced.* Or dead. Perhaps he did not like that you spoke with the Old Men; all those retired generals and politicians who keep interfering where they shouldn't. That won't last too much longer."

"You want to strike a deal?"

"Yes indeed. I want to let you live. It would prove so much more efficacious. And as you know, we neither of us wish to become bio-mechanically altered." He scowled at the thought. "So, my offer to you is this. No more claiming not to know anything about Robur's flying ship or Captain Nemo's submarine – though why anyone would travel trapped in a submerged boat is beyond me. You know so much, Mr. Turner. And you will share it with me and I will let you go. On the word of a gentleman."

Turner stared at him, trying not to laugh. Hetzel knew all about Nemo and the submarine. Cairo obviously wasn't spying for Hetzel anymore. "This is where I ask for a guarantee and you tell me that you're not offering a guarantee?"

"Quite the contrary. I will guarantee your safety once you have given me everything I want to know."

"Will this put you back in Hetzel's good graces?" Turner narrowed his eyes, looking for every telling twitch and grimace. Cairo had possibly broken with Hetzel completely.

Cairo complied by making a face. "Is it that obvious?"

"Indeed."

"Then, I will confess it. Your knowledge will make things quite right again. And it will give me all the more gravitas to explain away my decision to let you go. Surely that is a good deal?"

Turner folded his arms and narrowed his eyes. He looked to the locomotive and couldn't stop the chill running down his spine at the thought of being bio-mechanically enhanced to serve Hetzel. "Fine. Why not? I'm tired of keeping secrets for a man long dead." He used the chance to step closer to Cairo, lowering his head as he did, appearing quite unthreatening. "Robur betrayed me, so I'm not sure why I should protect his name."

The Egyptian was elated. "I was wondering the same thing. You owe him nothing."

Turner took the last step forward, with none of the men trying to stop him. His fingers seized on Cairo's cravat and Turner spun him around, slamming the little man's body into the two men immediately behind. Cairo squealed in response, with fury and flailing arms, but came up short of cursing Turner when he realized where his pistol had gone. Turner thumbed the hammer back and pointed it at the Egyptian. "I think I'll just leave."

"We had a deal!"

"No, sir. You offered a promise you weren't going to keep." He began edging his way around the front of the locomotive. He'd heard horses. All he needed was one, even if he was terrified of riding it. Chase the others away.

"Don't you dare!" Cairo had his one last card to play. One of the engineers was above and behind Turner, and didn't appear to have been seen yet. "You will never know what we've done to Robur. How we have saved him."

The effect on Turner was better than anticipated or desired. Turner stopped and stared, wide-eyed. "That, sir, is lie. Robur is dead." He saw the *Albatross* hit; saw her crash. Robur hadn't gotten out alive. The injuries Robur had suffered were too much. Not even Hetzel could put him together again after all that. It was a lie.

"I have not lied to you," Cairo said with false injury. "I'm not lying now. We have saved Robur the Conqueror and he is alive in Paris. But your pretty Doctor, well, that is all too bad. She shouldn't have been so eager to find you. One foolish woman who thinks she could best a man like Monsieur Hetzel and his agents."

"Of course you're lying. You're also providing a distraction, to give the man behind me time to attack, but I think that would be a bad idea." Turner barely glanced over his shoulder, eyes still on the Egyptian. "I don't think," he said to the engineer, "you want to take a bullet for Cairo."

Turner was wrong. The engineer leapt forward, taking Turner's bullet through his side. It didn't slow him down. The men crashed to the ground and wrestled for control of the pistol. No longer afraid for their own lives, the other men piled on, soon dragging Turner across the tracks toward Cairo who was sweating with fury. He stuck the sailor across the face and had to cower back when Turner almost got one of his fists free.

Blotting his face again, the Egyptian kept backing up, to insure his distance from Turner. "Put him out in front of this ... thing." He waved his hanky at the giant engine. "Let it run him over and we'll take the pieces of him to Mexico. I don't give a damn anymore."

As he was forced onto his knees, then face down across the rails, Turner could see that the little man was edging closer – still afraid to be within reach. Turner felt a searing hatred burning through his body that he couldn't act on. It was the comment about Robur. Why did he lie about Robur? And Lettie ... what had been done to her?

They rolled him on his side, facing the locomotive, and Turner's attention focused on the size of the pilot-catch, which might clear his body where the terrible wheels following would not. His hands were lashed down on the spar tie behind him, so that no one had to risk their own limbs to hold him in place, and his throat exposed across one of the rails. All but one man got off the track and walked away as if nothing of interest would happen.

As the engine hissed and shot hot grease, he knew it would be quick. The man that held his head by the hair would simply move out of the way at the last second. But it would all be over. Done.

He'd given nothing to them. He'd won. Yet, if they'd harmed Lettie, he'd lost – she'd lost, never mind him. He could never help her now.

The train blew two columns of steam out either side and showered the rail with sand just in front of the drive wheels, for traction.

A heated argument started up behind him; what did he care? The engine noise kept him from hearing the actual words but Cairo's voice kept getting louder and higher pitched. Was there a chance?

The wheels were clean and sharp, honed and polished by miles of grinding on the rails. Between weight and metal, they would cut through him in seconds. A single rivulet of water slid and twisted down the curve of the wheel looming in front of him until it could no longer resist the pull of gravity. Hesitating, it then pooled and fell.

As the last boiler steam was flushed and Turner was absolutely sure the locomotive was starting to move, he heard the Egyptian scream, "No!"

The train was not moving. There was a flurry of waving arms and men crowding around him. Someone let go of Turner's head and he curled his head off of the rail, still feeling the exposure on his neck. He wasn't happy that they were pulling him back up onto his feet –

there had been a sense of release in knowing that the questioning would finally come to an end. Yet, he felt a surge of relief that he wouldn't die like that: bloody and grotesque.

For a moment, all he saw was the hem of a black taffeta skirt as the wearer emerged from behind the locomotive.

The engineer shook his head. "Someone wants you to live, mister. Can't say that's the lucky draw ... 'Been better to die."

Turner silently agreed.

So ... superior technology hadn't solved some of the most basic travel discomforts of the country's rail lines: namely that poorly maintained tracks with uneven track joints that caused swaying and jerking. The most remarkable locomotive could not provide a passenger ... a prisoner ... a smooth opportunity to fall asleep. Not that Turner was likely to be slumbering under the circumstances, though he was numbingly fatigued.

Tied up and locked up again ... *again*! He *really* needed to do something about it – clearly he was not discouraging people enough from such actions. For the sheer amusement, he began a mental catalog of every way people had tried to restrain him, figuratively as well as physically in the last two decades. Lord, he had to be punch-dumb exhausted to be thinking like that.

His fingers tingled until he pumped his hands into fists to start the circulation again. Wrists held a shoulder's width apart, locked in irons attached to a beam above his head, only added to his exhaustion. Uncomfortable. Vulnerable. The Egyptian probably thought of that, angry as he was. Otherwise, Turner sat quietly in his chair.

The Egyptian would need to be dealt with. He'd spoken of Lettie, but had the comment been real? Was it a lie he told Turner to distract him? Well, he wasn't yet in a position to do anything about it.

The box car had been kitted out to serve as both storage and private office, which of course begged the question why it came complete with restraints. He sat in a low-backed chair, pine, uselessly slim cushion, sturdy legs, positioned under a beam of wood, in the middle of the car. Before him sat a carved desk with several cases and boxes, not to mention a single lamp. Behind it waited a high backed chair of exceptional comfort with its padded back, arms and seat – nearly a royal throne in mahogany. The space was designed for interrogation.

Why was it every one of his enemies felt the need to silence him – he wasn't prone to outbursts or to swearing. He could be brutally sarcastic but that hardly excused such abuse. There was no chance that he was going to start any sort of conversation, critical or elsewise. His captors had tied a cloth around his mouth. Why were people always doing that? The gag lay across the surface of his lips tightly, which in itself wouldn't prevent him from making noises or even shouting semi-coherently. It was a physical reminder to shut up and stay quiet.

Twice he squirmed to adjust his position; he'd been sitting too long without the option of moving. He shifted his back, to stretch slightly, as the car swayed. It was good that he was an experienced sailor as the motion of the fast moving train would make any landsmen ill. With each ankle chained to a chair leg, he couldn't move too much – just enough. Discomfort was a key ingredient in questioning a prisoner.

The door between the cars opened, behind him, allowing a rush of air and noise to envelop his chair.

The locomotive was at full throttle and careening down the track, headed somewhere he couldn't determine … yet. Flat ground – they had been at a fairly steep climb, but now they were on level terrain and making up for any lost time climbing what he assumed was a range of the Rockies. Cairo said something about Mexico. Oh hell, the Confederates he'd dealt with in California had made claims about Mexico. It made sense they were headed through the fairly empty, hidden valleys of the Rocky Mountains, toward the Rio Grande to the south.

The door closed and there was an uncomfortable relative silence. Turner stared forward, listening rather than looking to see what had come into the room. Allowing whomever the illusion that he was not fully interested in them appeared to be the first plan. Disinterest instead of fear. It would be most especially effective if it was Cairo again. Nothing would gall the little man more than being ignored. If he were upset, he might make mistakes.

For an eternal seeming moment, nothing but the train moved. A lantern bumped against the frame of the car. The wheels squealed and clicked on the track. The pumping hiss from the giant pistons on the engine created an almost lulling rhythm.

Taffeta?

A swish of deliberate steps with a trail of taffeta following across the floor boards.

Not a quick step, but a slow approach. Methodical.

A chair was moved into a position behind him. Probably a small chair such as the one he was sitting on.

Turner kept staring forward, though why he didn't look now, he couldn't decide. It was obviously not the Egyptian. Cairo wore strong cologne that would have wafted past Turner by now.

The taffeta sat down on the chair, and a warm breath brushed his ear. "It is a pity about your particular circumstances. Better than being overrun by the train, I think." The words were slow, carefully placed in an exact order, with a suggested satisfaction in them. A slight accent? Germanic. Northern Europe: Germany or Prussia. Only a minor accent, otherwise the pronunciation was exact. Educated. "You doubtless approve of our accommodations – *you* would not allow your enemy too much freedom. Most especially a talented saboteur, spy, and intelligencer such as yourself?" A woman's voice. Soft and arrogant. Confident. Slightly sweetened by a breathiness that was intriguing. Light, delicate, cold.

She reached around and slipped long, gloved fingers under his chin, with only the slightest hesitation. It was a rude gesture as people ought not to go around grasping at one another, and yet … yet Turner found it compelling. Her thumb rested on his covered lips. Why he didn't find it intolerable, as a gentleman should, confused him briefly. He was indeed a gentleman, as his father raised him to be, and despite all the actions in his past that suggested the contrary, he clung to the notion. It was unseemly for anyone to do this and he gently turned his head to remove it from her hand. Let's see where this is going, he decided.

The woman cooed a slight disapproval and instead of retreating, began examining his scar with her finger tips. That was too much and jerked his body away, and mumbling something sounding like "no."

She sighed this time and stood up. "I am too curious, Herr Turner. Your scar intrigues me." By the sound of the taffeta, she must have walked in a circle while considering her next question, then slid back into the chair behind him. This time leaning in to his right ear, she whispered, "were you alert the whole time? Did you feel the rope? What does it feel like … what does dying feel like?" Her questions were too enthusiastic. The tone in her voice suggested something almost aroused by the idea of his near execution and yet not an ounce of compassion at all.

Turner shot a look at her that spoke fully his feelings toward her question, and all the other hundred or so impertinent inquiries from callous curiosity seekers over the years. As if the experience of being hanged was one that a gentleman would go out to polite salons to lecture on? No one understood the damage that went well beyond a scarred neck or his thought that surviving was the worst outcome. Yet for a genteel woman, as he could see her clearly now, it was unconscionable for her to ask, let alone contemplate with such cheerful inquisitiveness.

As she'd caught his intense attention, she stood up gracefully and stepped back, holding out her arms as if showing her latest gown to her closest friends. Or was she showing him that she was unarmed yet still in control. Unafraid of him. "I see I am now worthy of your gaze. Good. You like what you see, yes? Though I think nothing of such an opinion and only care for my own approval, I am interested."

The suggestion that he would like what he saw tricked him into looking at her more closely – her entire intention. Golden red hair piled expertly on top of her head, harshly, with nothing covering her high forehead. Pale skin that that seemed to show the very physical workings of her body just beneath it. No color in her sharply angled cheeks. Brown eyes as deep in color as his blue eyes were intense. Long fingers on an elegant hand, covered in kid leather. Slender, corseted waist. Long and lean. Thin ruddy lips that held a frozen expression of heartlessness. She was a delicate flower carved from glacial ice or painted by an angry artist. Her clothing, her posture, her speech: all suggested upper-class birth.

Throat to floor, she was dressed in a perfectly tailored gown of black. Only a small relief of white lace encircled her neck and wrists. Somehow, he concluded this was her usual attire and not mourning weeds after all. Oh yes, this was the same woman from the Denver rail yard. The front of the dress was closed from a deep point to her chin with tiny black, glass buttons. A watch was pinned to her breast, the chain looping twice around her neck. She looked to be a crow, waiting to see what was dying and would become dinner.

A slight indentation – a line – cut across her cheek just under her right eye and was barely visible under a touch of powder which could only be seen when she passed directly into the sunlight streaming through breaks in the roofline.

He knew the look of a knife cut when he saw one.

But, how did a lady gain such an injury which reminded him of the facial scars some military men sported with pride. In fact, she had a formal, militaristic look to her.

"You intrigue me which is why you are still alive. You may call me 'Madame.' You do not need to be informed of my name. I come from a long line of excellent families, none of whom you will know; I hardly think the Turners of New England are part of our sphere. Were it not for the threats to my country," she sneered with deepening disdain, "I should be glad not to know anything of New England or any of the rest of this nation of commoners." Adding to an unknown audience, "or this dirty 'West' you people so admire. It is filthy, full of peasants and outcasts, racially inferior beasts, and there is not a decent hotel or person of intelligence to converse with."

Dirt is common to the desert, he spat back at her silently. Go home if you disapprove.

"You have had your look." She dropped her hands and strolled over to him, not losing her balance once despite the swaying of the car. Floating, with her skirts fluttering, her feet barely appeared to move at all. Elegantly, she sat on the edge of the table and spent a good minute artfully arranging the folds of her skirt. Carefully she removed her gloves and set them across her lap. She then looked to him with a bitterly frigid expression. "Quite simply, Herr Turner, I am very put out, but not entirely disappointed. I had hoped we would have captured the inventor, but I shall make myself satisfied with you. You haven't his capacity or brilliance, but you are mildly clever. And you have a few things I might find that make up for what you lack in intelligence." Those elegant hands reached around the back of his head and freed his mouth, the motion bringing her breasts close to his face. The woman smelled of French perfume. She casually tossed aside the gag. "There is no need for that thing anymore. Despite our being of very different spheres, we are going to be very great friends, you and I, for the next few minutes at least." She kept his head in her hands, sliding her fingers into his hair. "I want several things from you, but I want *this* first. And I will take it as it pleases me. Just like a man would, yes?"

In his entire life as a sailor, which had often led him to places a dignified person would not venture to, he had never known a lady of good birth to behave in such an ... an *unseemly* way. Her mouth bore down on his, cold, and she bit his bottom lip before sitting back to see his reaction. It had been something that vaguely resembled a kiss.

"You are silent, Herr Turner. Good. A common man should wait to speak until he has been given permission by his betters. I permit you, as I require information."

Finally he found the words. "I'm not going to ask what you want to know." Each syllable had to travel across the skin she'd assaulted, making it difficult for him to contain his anger, and bizarre interest. "I know what it is, as Mr. Cairo has already asked. As several others have already asked. No, I do not have secrets you can use to improve your technology."

"That is a lie." She might have giggled had she been able to produce a feeling or sense of humor to cause any such reaction. Her eyes were void of anything but calculation. "I expect that you will say whatever you need to say. You needn't worry. I have been warned by Admiral Hagen ..." She liked it when Turner's expression changed from fuming to caught off guard. "Do you remember Admiral Hagen? He is quite memorable, is he not?"

Turner refused to answer her, but yes – he remembered the Admiral. The Prussian commander of the airship *Albermarle II*. This did not bode well for him. Surprise, surprise. The Turner Luck was not going to show up when he needed it. Hagen had a bone to pick with Turner, especially after Turner scuttled his airship and left him in the wreckage. This was not good.

"The Admiral would not mind my taking your life, but we both understand what is at stake. I am not in a position to kill hundreds of soldiers and thus threaten you with their lives, as the Admiral did." Madame stood up and reached into a pocket in her skirt. "Thus I came prepared to extract the knowledge. Your reputation is that I would not get a satisfactory answer from you – voluntarily. Let us see what involuntary answers I might obtain. Deichgraef!" she shouted with only a minimum of effort.

Deichgraef came quickly when he was called. Turner got a quick look at him and immediately began assessing which of his bones the huge man would start breaking first.

He could only hold out so long. He had to think of something that would sound good enough but not be true. He wouldn't give them what they wanted.

The man behind Turner waited silently, easily bracing himself against the sway of the train. Broad. Ugly. His eyes were deeply set and slanted downward as if they had been pounded into that position. What hair he had was clipped to the shortest length on top of his head and altogether missing where eyebrows should have been.

From deep in her pocket, Madame withdrew a box. Small and rectangular, beautifully polished brass, it popped open easily in her hands. Not as crude or battered as the other boxes on the table. Setting it on the table, she lifted out two long, narrow, glass cylinders with a small amount of liquid in each. On either ends of the containers were handsome, textured caps made from bronze. One end had a plunger and the other a receptacle for a hollow needle, which she inserted skillfully in the first one. It caught a bit of light as she walked back toward him. "I won't waste my time by having the information beaten out of you – you probably still wouldn't give it to me and then all I'd have is no answer and a bloody corpse. There are much cleaner methods. Men generally don't like to use them because you are such brutes and prefer hitting and killing."

"Morphine?" Turner asked as casually as he could. "Opium?"

"The first mixture has not been named yet. It works very quickly. First you are you are acutely sensitive, then – when you can take no more pain – you become confused and submissive. The nerves become unbearably responsive ... Every touch is like a scalding knife." Slowly, a small trickle of the liquid was pushed out the sharp needle and into the palm of her hand. "It must be injected into your body." She looked to see Turner's reaction. "The other serum is Barbituric acid. I am told it is a by-product of apples and some unmentionable, natural wastes. A German scientist discovered this but did not recognize its potential, declaring it to have no medical use. I have found a different effect. It is somewhat anesthetic in small doses and entirely lethal in larger quantities. In between, a moderate dose makes a man a bit stupid and unable to create complex thoughts, such as lies." Turner did his best to seem unimpressed, which was not his true reaction. Hagen had warned her accurately about the man and what he'd been taught to do. He knew how to withstand a common interrogation, yet this was not quite the situation he'd been trained for. "Who knows, perhaps you will enjoy all this. I would like it if you did."

From behind, Deichgraef seized Turner's left arm, pushed the sleeve up, and held his elbow almost distended.

Madame approached. "Be happy I chose not to inject this into the vein in your neck. With your scar, I likely would not have found the right injection point without several attempts. You would think me cruel, and I would consider it inefficient."

Turner held still but turned his torso, forcing Deichgraef to stand closer behind him.

The back of Turner's head crashed into Deichgraef's forehead, causing the big man to stumble away.

The plan was simple: hold onto the chains around his wrists, kick out with the chair, and hope something would break. The chair, or the chair's leg. Or the needle in Madame's grip. Simple.

Deichgraef rushed back and grasped Turner's head, twisting it painfully, before Turner could do anything further.

"Nein! Do not kill him!"

Turner's arm was once again immobilized. Madame wrapped her own arm around him, and turning her back to him, jammed the needle into his arm. Despite all, Turner couldn't help it – he let out a howl and cursed. Twice more she stabbed at him. She was going to get lucky, but not before ripping his arm to shreds. Maybe he could still fight it. Maybe it wouldn't work. Finally Madame injected a dose that turned his arm numb almost immediately.

The big man let go, leaving Turner to drop back into his chair.

Madame gripped his head by the hair and looked into his eyes, excited to see how quickly or slowly the drug might work on him. In moments, his eyes blurred and his ears filled with the sounds of a raging ocean. His exertions had made his blood pump and pushed the poison into his heart and head too fast.

She let go of him in annoyance and stepped back to watch him slump in his chair. Picking up her gloves, which had been knocked from the desk during the brief scuffle, she dusted them off. Her hair was disheveled and there would be no opportunity to make it right again. She slapped him across the face with the gloves, but he didn't feel it. Not yet. The drug needed to take longer if it was to work at all.

How rude, he thought as his breathing became labored and dizziness overwhelmed him. A member of an "excellent family" should know how to behave better. He must have said it out loud – the gloves struck him across the face a second time.

Had someone shoved a burning torch into his face, it would have hurt less. Turner gasped at the pain and recoiled as far as his restraints would allow him, stunned by the effect of the drug.

Madame smiled so slightly that it might not have been noticeable in another circumstance. She walked back to him, resting her hand on the desk for balance, her skirts dragging along with her. With a wave of her hand, she sent Deichgraef to the back of the box car to watch. That was his job – to watch. Slowly, she spotted Turner squirming in his clothing, as even contact between his shirt and skin was causing exceptional discomfort.

Deichgraef said nothing as he glared from the rear of the car, noting how smoothly she moved. Madame slid away from the desk and sat down on Turner's lap. To him, she must have weighed as much the train. Meticulously she observed the strange combination of pain and pleasure as she stroked his hair or ran her finger across his throat. When she kissed him this time, he was at once repulsed and aroused, the combination she desired. Her satisfaction never showed on her face. He was after all a "thing." A source of information. An intriguing experiment. As handsome as he was, his looks did not compensate for his being of low birth and undistinguished military career – two inexcusable failures. He had no breeding or blood to have pride in.

Turner was having considerable difficulty breathing, she finally noticed. That was one of the risks of the drugs. It would add to his sensation of fear and panic. He was alive and that meant he could be of use. He had skills and knowledge. She kissed him again, without passion, and allowed her hands to explore the shape of his chest. He was strong. A laborer. Good for farming but little else. Or in Turner's case, good for working aboard a ship.

"Now, Herr Turner. You will discuss with me your life after the War but before today. I desire to know all about Robur and you will tell me."

Her hand stopped on the pouch resting on his breast. "Is this what they call a 'Medicine Bag'? One of those dirty Indian things?" She lifted it up to inspect it closely. A simple leather pouch, with a small amount of embellishment, on a leather cord. "Is this where you keep your good luck, Herr Turner?" With a hard yank that sent searing pain shooting in all directions from the point where the pouch's cord touched his neck, she tore the pouch away and threw it down on the desk.

Had she opened it and examined it, she would have found only ashes. He'd done right by Lettie and it gave him a brief, delicious moment of hope. The hope vanished the instant Madame picked up a sharp, polished metal instrument.

Cairo sat in the passenger car hating the luxury. Normally he would be quite satisfied with himself amongst lovely padded chairs, crystal decanters of expensive liquors, and fringed curtains. He had a job to do and he couldn't do it locked out from Turner's questioning. It was intolerable. He was very good at such things, though he did tend to do more of the talking.

The giant locomotive had stopped for water. It wasn't precisely invulnerable. It still needed water and greasing every 150 miles. So there he sat, watching the dust settle on everything and waiting for the train to start moving again, with nothing to occupy him but his angry thoughts.

It was not right that ... *that woman* was doing his job. Yet it was the price he had to pay for aligning himself with the Prussians and this New Confederacy. Perhaps he would steal into the car and see what was left of the awful Yankee. Perhaps she wouldn't mind if he watched, and he would even go so far as to promise not to say a word. Just so he could see that horrid man get what he deserved.

When the door opened, he fully expected to see the woman and readied his request to observe Turner's interrogation. Instead, the bulky Deichgraef barged into his solitude. "Oh, it's you."

"Ja," Deichgraef replied, less impressed with Cairo than Cairo was with him.

"I assume Mister Turner is providing you with the information you desire."

"Nein. Not yet. He is willful and used to hiding things." The Prussian poured himself a drink, which Cairo thought was presumptuous. Deichgraef was an employee ... a servant, as it were. "She is enjoying her task. I think we would be wise to leave her to it." It was as if the Prussian knew what Cairo was thinking.

"He's dangerous. You should kill him the minute he has given you what you want. And I insist on observing his death. I want to ensure that he actually dies." Cairo began digging into his pockets to find a handkerchief. "It would be just like him to live. Very rude of him not to expire as required."

Deichgraef hissed something that might have been a laugh, through his nostrils. "I will see to it he is very dead. With all the Confederate sympathizers here, I'm sure we'll have quite a crowd for his execution."

Cairo shook his head. "They're fools, you know. They think only of revenge."

"Agreed." The Prussian saluted Cairo's point with his glass before swallowing the contents whole. "They have no idea of anything beyond their small ambitions. To raise a South that never really existed? Slavery? Plantations? Pride? Why should they have any? What have they ever done but fail miserably, at the expense of many including my country, all in support of an economy that was collapsing when they started their absurd war? Had they fought the war as we told them to, and used the weapons we gave them, they would have won. Now look at them." He callously swept his hand across the curtains to reveal a team of workers outside the train. "Tattered uniforms. Burning hatred to fuel them. Wrapping themselves in a flag that lost its honor two decades ago..." The workers, he noted, were finishing the latest changes to the locomotive with haste.

In daylight, they couldn't sit in the open.

Cairo perked up. "You have no intention of handing the reins of power over to them." He was almost delirious with his discovery. "You have convinced them to fight the war again, but when it comes time, it will be Prussia not a New Confederacy that will rule the western coast." He was ready to jump up and down, were it not so hot in the car. "Naturally, you will debilitate them from the inside, making any future resistance to your establishment of a government impossible. This is too wonderful. I am deeply approving of the skill and cunning of the plan. Your government must consider me your humble but enthusiastic admirer. And, I will see that dreadful man, Turner, die. Truly this must be an auspicious occasion."

Deichgraef said nothing. He poured himself another glass and saluted again.

"We're heading south ... I can tell." Turner spoke through the remaining haze of chemicals racing through his bloodstream. The rocking of the train had started again, which meant they were on the move again. He wasn't entirely sure, but that sort of made sense.

"Southwest," Madame commented grudgingly. "We have come into the New Mexico Territory. It is as filthy as Colorado."

Turner expended enough energy to lift his head. "Why?"

"The last dosage must be wearing off. You are asking questions now? "

"Why not?" he said with a lopsided smile not meant for her.

"Limitations *you* inflicted on us. It is your fault we must take this route."

The serum still blockaded any complex problem solving, and with exasperation, Turner let his head drop. "I think ... under the circumstances ... you might want to explain it to me."

She looked at him for an uncomfortably long, intense time. She watched him struggle to remain in control of himself. It was pleasing. "You destroyed our means of air travel – the dirigible *Albermarle*. It was designed as a means to carry this vehicle over the mountains and across great distances not otherwise connected by rail lines."

"So, you're stuck on the rails that exist. Lines that other people are using. You might be seen." He gesticulated with little purpose; his left hand had been freed so that he could tend to certain needs but otherwise he was still restrained. It didn't matter – the drugs had incapacitated him.

Madame nodded slowly. "In a while, this limit will no longer exist. Your mind is indeed starting to work properly again. Perhaps I should give you another injection." Turner's controlled reaction was satisfying – of course he would not want more. "Or perhaps I shall leave you partially coherent for the time being." And there was no doubt that too much of the serum could easily kill him which would be a waste. He hadn't told her everything yet. She would have to be careful not to overdose him. "Here in this territory, we will switch to the line that leads into Arizona, another territory of yours, to some ridiculous place called 'Bisbee', then to Douglas. From there we will use an American line being built through Mexico from Douglas to a little known mining town called Nacozari. Tucked away in the mountains where few people go."

"Building a couple more of these … things?"

"As many as we can. The mines are convenient for obtaining important elements in our manufacturing … but why should you worry about this?"

"We're going south. Not my favorite direction."

He pulled as hard as possible. Sweat, mixed with blood and the Turner Luck that he'd been put back in his restraints in a sloppy fashion, had given him one possible opportunity. His wrists chafed as he twisted them; something was going to come loose. He was ready to chew his hand off if that was what it would take.

They were headed south. This was not tolerable.

The pounding and clanging outside was tremendous. In the fading light, crews were doing something beyond simple repairs and greasing. They had only a short amount of time before nightfall and the need for bright lights to work under. Lights meant that they were detectable; something the locomotive was designed to avoid.

He barely remembered, yet Madame happily recounted to him the information he couldn't stop from slipping out of his lips. Lightning. Robur wanted to use lightning. How was it stored? He wasn't clear – honestly, he didn't understand the technology. Multiple screws for stabilizing the airship. He'd been about to respond to the question of building materials for Robur's airship when they had to make a stop. Madame wasn't disappointed. She was looking forward to continuing their "friendly discussions." He wasn't going to survive many more.

He was running out of time and options.

His head was clearing. It was the lingering serum that dulled his reactions and ability to falsify or significantly alter his knowledge that worried him. He was certain she was doling out the doses carefully, hoping not to overwhelm and kill him.

Turner tugged again.

His hand slid down inside the manacle to the first joint of his thumb. He yanked and jerked his arm until his hand came free, leaving a small amount of flesh behind. As much as the wound stung, it was nothing compared to the drugged pain he'd survived and he gladly left the tissue behind as a sacrifice to the gods.

The noise from outside the car was enough that he could break the chair and free his legs without drawing attention. It was a move that took more effort than he'd imagined, but hurt a bit less than he'd expected.

Turner grasped the broken chair leg in one hand and fumbled along the length of the desk. His pouch was there, and he snatched it away from the desk to shove it into his pocket.

Someone was standing on the platform off the back of the car. Not a usual design feature for box cars but then few box cars had elegant desks and interrogation equipment. It was likely Deichgraef.

Turner waited, listening, trying to hear over the pounding work outside.

Deichgraef, or whomever it was, walked down the two small steps and away. Turner heard the man's feet scrape on the gravel and kick away rocks on the ground. Slowly, Turner opened the door, looked for anyone lingering on the platform, then leaned out further to see if anyone was near the rear of the car.

In the twilight, he had a good chance of slipping away, though he doubted they would leave the area without knowing that he was safely locked up. Finding he wasn't, they would search, but by then the night would blacken the sky and Turner could disappear in the darkness. And the drugs might wear off by then.

He stepped silently onto the ground and peered around the side of the car. What he could see made no sense. The wheels were being linked together in groups. Ball joints had been installed since he'd first seen the locomotive in San Francisco, yet their use was a mystery. Each time they had stopped to take on water or to re-grease the joints, several workers had sprung into action, unloading new parts and enhancing the locomotive. Surely, by the time they reached the border, whatever changes were engineered into the behemoth would be complete? Men shouted to one another while hefting a new axle into place between the sets of wheels. Would such separations make the locomotive run more smoothly?

Laying on the side of the road was a strange type of wheel: he knew what they were. Dreadnaught wheels. On a single, possibly continuous link. The British had used such an oddity during the Crimean War, but had discovered the hard way that the "Megatherium War Horse" couldn't maneuver in soft ground or slippery hills. This was unique. With little effort on the part of the operators, Turner guessed, they could be loaded up over the existing rail wheels, widening their tread. But why? Did it matter? He'd have time to think it out, once his head cleared.

One thing was clear, he wouldn't be able to able to get past so many men until it grew a little darker out. The terrain was bleak with few places he could establish a defensive position. Rolling hills with short, round shrubbery could provide no protection against gunfire. Sandy soil was difficult to run in. And despite his doubtful ability to ride a horse, he would gladly do so – clinging to its tail if he had to – if only there were horses to be had. His options at first inspection were nonexistent.

Telling himself that he was reluctant to go back to the interrogation car to wait was an understatement. The truth was that inside the car, he had advantages. But, if he went back, the first thing he needed to do was locate the box of Madame's serum and destroy it. Even if that meant he was forcing their hand immediately – his death was the only possible outcome if he could not escape. He could not reveal another one of Robur's secrets. And there was the matter of Lettie. It could only be a matter of time before they started asking about her. Cairo would insist.

He was beginning to hate that desk. Staring at it as he re-entered the car, he concluded it was gaudy, ridiculous, and ...

Madame's boxes sat on top. One by one, Turner opened them. Some had hideous looking medical instruments; others had small knives and pins. Perhaps he'd gotten off lightly? Finally, he located the fancy box with the two cylinders in it.

Correction, he noted, one cylinder. Where ...?

A heavy arm slammed down on his shoulders, flattening him against the top of the desk. Turner rolled and struck out with the chair leg he'd kept in hand. Deichgraef's head recoiled from the blow. He shook it off and threw his weight on top of Turner. For a man of his size and heft, he had been stunningly silent creeping up on the sailor. Now he held nothing back, grasping Turner's head in his big hand and shoving him brutally against the desk again. The contents of the second cylinder were shot into Turner's neck and he was flipped over onto his back. Turner pounded the Prussian twice more with the chair leg, drawing a cascade of blood from cuts to Deichgraef's forehead. There was little else he could do. They stared at each other.

"You're a quiet bastard, for someone that big," Turner said, slipping off the desk, onto the floor, feeling the effects of the serum rush through his body.

Taffeta? Did she always wear taffeta, he thought in a haze. Madame stared down at him, with Cairo leaning out from behind her. She almost looked sad. "How much did you give him?"

"All that was left."

"Hmm. Well, that will either kill him or leave him useless for a whole day."

Cairo glared down at Turner. "I hope it does not kill him. It would be too easy for him."

Pushing the Egyptian back, Deichgraef interrupted, "We have no more serum and no more time, Madame. Have you learned enough?"

She sighed, inspected Turner one last time with her eyes, and declared, "yes. I believe we have learned all we can from Herr Turner. It is too bad." She rested a finger on his chin. "Herr Cairo, you have been wanting to put an end to this man's life for some time now. You will see to it."

The Egyptian was about to over-enthusiastically leap into the situation, when Deichgraef threw his proverbial blanket over his fire. "We cannot stay long enough to do anything ... convoluted. I will see to it."

"No." Cairo said lingeringly. "This is for me to do. I want to see him hanged ... again."

"Go with Madame," the Prussian barked his order. "This is bloody work and I will do it."

"First you deny me the chance to watch his questioning and now I cannot see him die?" His whine was childlike, as though the whole situation was a game with no real consequences.

Madame walked away from Turner, nearly forgetting him in the same gesture. "Come now, Herr Cairo. We must not soil ourselves with business that is not immediate to our attention." Stopping for a moment, she looked at him, recognizing something between them. Was that disappointment?

Taffeta. It made that particular sound, Turner thought. What ... did they ... call it? What did they ...

Turner kept slamming his fists into the boards that enclosed him. It wasn't very helpful – none of the nails were loosening. Dust was falling onto his face and his cough could not be stifled. He held his breath nearly choking on the dirt.

In that moment of desperate silence, he could hear nothing beyond a relentless rolling of wheels on ill-travelled road.

They hadn't heard him – yet. They probably thought he was still unconscious. Part of him wished he was. The drug wasn't wearing off as gracefully as it before, if one called that graceful.

Carefully, he allowed shallow, almost useless breaths to steal into his lungs.

Someone cursed as their horse slipped on the gravel.

It took him a while to clear his head. The jostling wagon bed didn't help. Nothing made sense at first. Then it came back to him: this was the Egyptian's doing. Madame only wanted him killed. Anything convoluted was likely the invention of the angry little Cairo.

Cairo's plan might take too long; the cold alone was going to kill him.

The whole wagon jolted hard as it hit rocks, dropped into holes, and generally struck every deformation in the road. Gravel popped out from under the wheels and hooves. Mules protested the rugged road and steep terrain. Now and then, the driver cursed at the road.

The road to where?

He'd been unconscious. Good thing. He'd never allowed them to put him into a box had he been able to fight. It was that damn chemical the woman shot into his veins. The sound of arguing voices were familiar, but his brain was not set to right yet.

Clean air, his lungs craved air!

Suddenly the wagon stopped. Not a good sign. The box was lifted up and unceremoniously dumped off the back of the wagon.

Turner's mind raced through every horrible outcome: burial alive or being left to freeze to death.

He bit into the gag still stuffed inside his mouth. His hands were still bound, and so too were his legs as far as he could tell; he couldn't move them.

And they'd put him in his coffin prematurely – from his point of view. Twice he'd tried forcing the nailed lid, ramming his hands against it. But with little to no space to move in, the gesture was useless. Pressing his hands against the boards, he pushed. His head was spinning from the drug still. If it could, his chest would explode.

The wagon driver called out to a man who was, by the sound of things, riding a horse nearby. "There it is," he cried out. "I think …"

No more time. Twice more he rammed his hands into the lid. Each time it lifted slightly, allowing streaks of light inside, but seemed to lock back down into place and sink him into darkness.

"Where the hell is it?"

He recognized the voice of one of the Egyptian's men. Probably the tall, lanky man with sun-dried leathery skin and a permanent squint to his eyes.

"Where the hell is this mineshaft? Don't they mark nuthin' round here?"

"Ain't no point," said the tall man's stouter companion. "They're all abandoned around here. Silver's been played out. No point in stayin'."

Turner could barely hear them, but the important words penetrated his drugged haze. "Silver." That was an important description. The word "mineshaft" however was turning his stomach.

"Don't see why we gotta' bother with this whole thing. Leave 'em here. What's he gonna do?"

A deep voice replied, "Shut up and do as you are told." The accent was thick and memorable. Deichgraef.

The box was lifted by the three men who complained about the work incessantly. They picked up the box and carried it uphill; moving quickly and not in unison. One man barely held up his end and it dragged slightly each time he insisted on taking a break.

Sound and fractional light changed to complete darkness and echoes. The temperature plunged dramatically. They were inside the mineshaft. Their steps echoed against narrow walls and large stones were kicked out of the way.

"He ain't big, why's he so heavy?"

"Shut up! We ain't got far to go. They couldn' pump fast enough and the whole thing jus' filled. Been like that all o're the place. Ain't no more money in Tombstone. No more silver. Jus' whores 'n drunk cowboys."

"Was' wrong with that?"

Tombstone.

Turner raced to make his mind summon up the memory. Something he'd read in San Francisco. Something about a feud and a gunfight. Thirty seconds of shooting and a year or two of infamy. Tombstone got its name in the papers.

His captors stopped. Deichgraef stepped back. "This will do."

Turner braced himself. Would they bury him? Would they just leave him there? After everything he'd lived through, could his luck still be that good? If they left him, he could get out. He would find a way. Damn it, he hadn't survived this long – against all the odds – to die like this.

The box was stood on one end by the two cowboys, dragged, and then pushed over the edge of some precipice. Down the steep decline it fell then slid a significant distance, splashing foot first into water and mud.

The water flooded into his box and up to his waist. This time, a curse burst out of Turner's lungs, only muffled slightly by the gag.

"He's awake."

"Don' matter none."

"It's stuck – it ain't sinkin'," the man shouted, an echo of his voice warbling for a moment after.

Deichgraef cleared his throat. Such a sound was threatening.

"I ain't goin' down there to un-stick it. You go. I ain't paid 'nuff to do it. It's movin' anyway."

The box was moving.

Slowly, but unquestionably, it was moving. Turner stopped struggling. Every movement encouraged it to sink further with more water rushing in.

Think!

"We're done 'ere. We did our job."

"Tolerably," Deichgraef said, the sound of his voice floating back as he started down the tunnel toward the entrance.

"We could go to town. Get ridda that fella and have ourselves a right time of it."

The second cowboy didn't speak.

All Turner could hear was his own muffled desperation and the spinning of a revolver's cylinder.

Their footsteps away from him were distinct, accentuated by cracking gravel and curses at how hard it was to walk up and out. They continued to argue with one another until neither their voices nor wagon could be heard.

Slow your breath. Deeper. Control.

The box slipped five inches lower before sticking in the mud again. The water line was up to his chest and making his breathing more difficult than it already was. A sailor's worst nightmare – drowning.

Perhaps, after all, they *had* done their job well enough?

Freezing water. It kept rising. Or the box kept sinking. Again and again he pushed or twisted his body to force the lid.

Death had been chasing Turner and now had caught up.

His fingertips went numb. So too did his feet.

His lungs burned. There was little difference between this and being strangled ... hanged ... There were memories he thought he'd pushed away. Andersonville prison. The horrors of being a prisoner of war, in the hands of the Confederacy. They were nothing but meat, possibly to be traded for Southern officers, but otherwise to be ignored or abused. For trying to escape, for doing what he had to do, for leading the attempt, he'd been sentenced to death. Hanging had not killed him. Disease and starvation had not killed him. The whole of the Confederacy could not take his life. But that was the old Confederacy. Now there was a new one and he could no longer do anything to stop it.

... It was over ...

His life ... oh God what a life he'd led ...

... It was over ...

... No! He had to live!

He had to survive. Lettie. Lettie Gantry. If for no one else, nothing else, he had to live. He had to win against an enemy that was not his alone.

The box slid again, this time leaving only the tiniest space of air. Sound muted to a horrible sloshing and bubbling din: the pressure of the water tightened around his ears. Filthy water filled his nose, leaving a stench inside.

One more try...

1884
The Mine
Arizona Territory

A howling wind blew down the narrow mineshaft, echoing its ugly roar against the abused and ravaged rocks that once held treasure for its owners. Empty. Abandoned.

A perfect location to misplace a dead body.

In the late 70s, silver veins were found running beneath the red and beige dirt that typified the American southwest territories. Anyone who had neither sense nor fear of continued failure had flocked to the region, some even coming as far as the hopeless California gold fields. It had taken the Sierra Nevada mountains decades to burn out the energies of young fortune hunters. The Arizona mines were played out, as it was called, in under a decade. Some left for Colorado and the silver hiding in the Rocky Mountains; some drank away their lonely nights; some gambled off their mine shares – sometimes happier to lose.

The silver was expensive to mine to begin with. But when the aquifer was breeched, the flood waters came and the hopes of riches left. Of course, the more stubborn miners tried pumping out the water, but it too was expensive – making Arizona silver not worth the effort.

Some went south into Mexico to seek their fortunes there.

Some changed professions, and not always to what was best.

Some headed north to the Yukon or Alaska.

Some died there. It was rumored that more than a few mines held the remains of its owner, neatly shrouded after their demise and coffined properly. Such mines became broken men's mausoleums – temples to their failures.

Yet another mine, with a coffin found buried in mud or sunken in the flood water, was nothing too exciting for the local residents. It was to be expected. And if the body inside seemed to be that of a stranger, well that too could be explained. Some of the mine owners were practically unknown to their neighbors. Besides, with outlaws and Indians ransacking the country, bodies cropping up were part of the daily routine.

A pair of fists burst through the surface, followed pieces of wood and loosened nails, then a face ... gasping for breath. He disappeared back under the water for only a second or two before struggling to lift his face higher each time. Finally, Turner pushed himself out of the box and into the slick mud.

With still-bound hands, he grasped at the sides of the incline and pulled himself up inch by inch, by any portion of the structure that would hold him. His legs were not entirely responsive, and he couldn't rely on them until he could get warm. Yet once out of the icy water, the interior heat of the mine helped him. Outside the mine, the temperature was frigid.

Finally, he reached the top of the incline and the long passage back out to civilization ... or not. Wet and exhausted, Turner left himself lying vulnerably on the mineshaft floor. He gulped air and wiped thick mud off his face.

The mine was oddly wide – perhaps it had been a cave or the miners had created a staging area. To his left were the broken tracks for the hauling cart. Behind him, it seemed the mine floor had collapsed, taking a portion of the rails with it, then filled with water.

Just his luck. The Turner luck. He was still alive but far from any destination he'd intended. Grinding the knot of the rope around his wrists, which he could see in the blinding white light shining in from the outside, he struggled to free his hands. The mud and the water helped. The hemp shredded after a time and finally let him go. Slowly he rolled onto his back, allowing the thick tasting air fill his mouth and lungs.

He had to get dry somehow. Well, there was enough broken wood lying around. Trying desperately not to shiver, he saw what he needed ... ah, the Turner luck ... an old lantern. Inside it was not the chemical mixture that was so common, but good, old fashioned, kerosene. Plenty of rocks to strike a spark, and kindling.

Such a task was easier to read about than to accomplish, but he was determined. The pain in his fingers only forced him to work harder.

It paid off. Slowly, it paid off.

Turner began to free himself from any remaining bonds and to scrape off the mud from his coat sleeves. A broken axe handle would serve as his only weapon. His fire was far enough away from the cold entrance that no one would see the light burning. He'd meant to stay awake, on guard. But slowly his mind refused to be conscious once he'd concluded they were probably not coming back for him. Certainly not tonight, he decided.

He didn't exactly remember stoking or refueling the fire, but somewhere in the night, he had. By morning he'd even tossed the handle into the flames. It was better as firewood anyway. Most of him was recovering from the exposure – something the pain informed him of. He was still damp in quite a few places but mostly dry.

He couldn't stay. Someone would come back to check, he was sure. If not the Egyptian, then the Woman or Deichgraef.

Stepping out into the sunlight, he could see that he was on a hillside covered in thick desert shrubs and twisted cholla cactus skeletons, ghost flowers embracing the chilled air in splashes of tan against acres of sage green, and curl leaf mountain mahogany twisting its gray branches into gnarled fingers reaching out to snag a lost soul. Snow had fallen not long ago but could not last in the sunlight. Only in protected patches under trees or cacti waited the last frozen piles of ice. It was a good thing: Turner could use those patches of snow for water.

In the distance he could see a wall of mountains, black in silhouette against the burning white sunrise. Turner had no idea which mountains they were. But people, he concluded, tended to homestead or to build towns at the base of mountain ranges, where water pooled or flowed into the valley. His best path would be to head in that direction. Northeast. Into the sun.

He was lost.

No matter the reason he could apply to direction or human habitation possibilities, he was lost. And alone. He shouldn't have been. He was vulnerable and the chances were too good that he could do more harm than the Old Men's letters. It was unwise for him to go it alone, but what choice did he have? Would have? Should have?

He let go; of what, he didn't care. He simply let go.

Silence.

All the swirling, colliding thoughts vanished in the face of the emptiness he stood in. The worries of men seemed so small compared to the vast sweep of the hill and explosion of light on towering cacti and a desert in full bloom.

Turner stood still for a long time. At first he watched his breath condensing into wisps of fog, visible proof he was still alive. The quiet of the morning was pleasing. For the last few months he had been on a noisy ship with civilian passengers, in crowded hotels, trapped inside a military airship with crews working constantly, on trains that clacked and rumbled down their tracks. This ... this was the first time in so long that he had no other sound beyond the wind and the voices of his mind. And those voices were awestruck into silence.

The wind was strong and cold, and it changed its tune as it raced through different structures. The entrance to the mine produced a low growl and the occasional groan of wood resisting the forces exerted on it. The sharp twigs and branches of the shrubs tricked the mind into hearing water flowing over rocks. Sand swept up and out across the hillside hissed. Occasional pebbles loosened and popped out of their eroding, dried-mud settings.

The flowing hills around him had been sculpted into domes and sugar-loaves by the same wind and much time. Their dry sandstone and broken layers of compressed rock would have blown away long ago were it not for the tenacious desert plant life. Stripes of dusty rose and rich purple burst through the desert greens, saturated with the colors only to vanish in the coming week or two. The desert spring was always short.

This was, perhaps, the first time Tom Turner could define "peace" in a very long while. He'd known it occasionally, when steering the *Albatross* through the clouded atmosphere, alone in the wheel house, spared the company of the other crewmen. But this ... this was different.

He'd have a long way to walk to get to a town or a homestead, he decided. Sticking his bare hands under his arms after pulling up his collar, he looked out at the possible road, his eyes following the obvious wagon ruts frozen in the thin layers of sand and disappearing snow.

At first, he found each step to be difficult. He didn't want to leave this place of peace and silence. The bitter ache in his hands warned him he couldn't remain in the winter chill for very long, even with the sun rising above the ridgeline.

Slowly, he walked, his shadow stretched out behind him. His mind was nowhere nearby. Turner thought of his father, long gone. He remembered a particularly cold night in the Northeast when gales blew in from the sea: how his father put a blanket over his shoulders and stirred up the coals a little more. He remembered the sea stories that were told that night and how his father had briefly mentioned his mother, of whom neither spoke, as though hearing her name would summon up a ghost neither was prepared to know of.

He found a road, or rather something akin to a road. More wagons had passed along its route than the path he'd just left. On the hill there were more signs of abandoned mines, rusting equipment squealing and creaking in motion.

Turner stepped out onto the better road and started down the hill, always noting the location of the distant mountains.

The wind stayed by his side, rocking heavy twigs and swaying the arms of various cacti, whose flowers had begun to open. The desert was really quite beautiful in the spring. After a bend in the road, the wind prodded him in the back, urging him on as he became lost again in his memories. Lettie was foremost in thoughts. So too was the offer to rejoin the military, to serve once again.

At the arroyo, which blessedly had the remnants of a stream flowing through it, he stopped to drink the coldest, clearest water he'd ever had. The wind never left him, and every now-and-again, he felt as though it wanted to pick him up and carry him away. He'd gladly go, anywhere it took him. His body seemed to be light. Yes, he could just float on the wind like a leaf.

The horse snorted.

The lever action of the rifle was distinctive.

For some reason, he honestly didn't care who was back there. He raised his hands and dared to look over his shoulder. People were sneaking up on him too much lately. Or ... perhaps he was letting them for reasons he didn't understand yet. His senses and his reactions were still sluggish. So much for floating away.

The man from the wagon was obviously afraid of Turner and more than just a bit jittery in general. The surprise of finding anyone out in the hills was enough to recall every feeling of paranoia he'd ever know. He shouted again at the man he'd forced to remain on his knees, his hands near his head. "I am not a patient man. Who sent you!"

"Sir, I have not been sent by ..."

"I'd be in my rights to shoot you."

Turner waited patiently to see if the man had anything more to say. When the pause in the conversation seemed long enough, he took a deep breath – something he valued quite a bit after the week's events – and calmly replied. "Sir, I am lost out here. I do not know anyone. I am not here to do anything. I was brought here and I am hoping you will either choose to help me or to just leave me."

"Sayin' you aren't a Cowboy?"

He tried not sounding sarcastic. "I don't have any equipment or a horse, and I don't recall seeing cattle nearby. If I'm a cowhand, don't you think I'm a fairly pathetic one by the looks of things?" God, he tried not to sound rude but he really was in no mood for this. His knees were starting to hurt from the rocks he was kneeling on.

"You're wet. In places, I can see you're wet. You got mud all over you." The man's voice had dropped to a lower volume but Turner didn't doubt that the gun was still pointed at his back. "Where've you been all night?"

"At the bottom of a mine, trying not to drown. I crawled my way out, though I swear I don't know how."

"The mines are nearly all played out now. Other than a few company places, I'd say there aren't any single mines still worth operating. What did you expect to see?"

He wanted to put his hands down. "It wasn't what I wanted to see, it was what someone else wanted to see – me – dead." The wind wasn't going to pick him up and take him anywhere, but it was going to blow consistently. And the man was right, Turner was still wet in some places, which he could feel more intensely now. "I managed to get out, and I managed to dry off a bit, but I'd like to not freeze to death if it's all the same to you." He heard the man jump down from the wagon. That was not good news. That usually happened just before the gunman shot – an action to get him closer to the intended target, to guarantee he wouldn't waste a bullet by missing.

Instead the man walked in a wide circle around Turner to get a better look at him.

Turner finally got to see who was threatening him. A tall fellow; decently dressed. Sandy brown hair and beard. An expensive hat and gloves. A well used rifle. Clean shoes. Polished. Maybe in his mid to late 40's. He didn't have a killer's look, but then, Turner could be wrong.

"What's your name, Mister?"

"Thomas Turner. I don't suppose you'll tell me yours?"

"John Clum. Editor of the Tombstone *Epitaph*. Former Mayor. Don't let that fool you, I know how to fight. Been bringing in Indians and outlaws for my better share of life. Want to put your hands down?" When Turner nodded slowly, Clum gestured that he could. "Now that I look at you, you seem to have been through plenty." He paused while staring at Turner's scar, gripped his rifle a little tighter, but otherwise showed decent decorum by not mentioning the disfigured skin. "You say someone put you down a mineshaft? Well, that's a new story to me. I can't say I believe you, but then, there's room here for the truth. Get yourself up."

As Turner forced his body to comply, he moved very carefully. The last thing he needed was a bullet hole. "If you please, I'd like to get to the nearest town, which I presume is Tombstone, or so I overheard. You don't have to take me – I won't impose on you – but if you could point me in the right direction, I would be very grateful."

After a moment's thought, Clum shook his head. "No, I won't leave you out here. It's more than a couple of miles and you won't make it on foot. Now see here, you're going to drive us. I'll stay in back where I can watch you, and I'll give you directions."

"Drive? The horses?" Turner looked over at the horses, which he quickly decided were laughing at him. Horses and he – they didn't get along too famously. He always felt they had other plans for him and no intention of telling him what those were. He'd only vaguely achieved a truce with a horse back on Hawaii.

"You got a problem with that?"

"Yes, sir. I ... well that is to say ..." He was directed to climb up on to the seat. "Frankly sir, I don't know how." He picked up the reins and stared at them. "I've never driven a wagon in my whole life. Now, if you want me to put up a sail, I know how to do that."

"A sailor? In the middle of Arizona? You're a bit landlocked."

"Yes, sir. Believe me, I know."

"You bring a man in here at gunpoint and he gives me that bull story – I'm supposed to believe he was near to murdered?" The man said, expecting absolutely no objection to his challenge. He had little to say, thus when he said it; he knew that he would be heard. He removed the badge and set it on the table.

"Slaughter, I understand your feelings, but I couldn't just leave him there. Turner here says that there are men who tried to kill him out there, possibly come to town. Weren't they, Mr. Turner?"

Turner's head was pounding and he realized he hadn't eaten in a day nor had he had any coffee. The food waiting on the marshal's desk was a few hours old, but would still prove quite tasty – he would not turn it down. He doubted the man would offer him anything.

"Answer up, mister. I ain't got all day and I have to explain what happened to you to the real marshal." The man's lips barely moved but the tone was clear. "It's bad enough I have to pay off my debt by holding down the fort here, but I am not going to get caught up in some mischief without knowing what I've gotten into."

It was possible part of his headache came from the Texas drawl Slaughter had, the sound of it triggering all sorts of ugly, wartime feelings. The man was of the right age, too, to have been fighting for the South. Still, that was Turner's head filling in the gaps of his understanding, fostered by pain and exhaustion. It wasn't likely, but what if this fellow supported the New Confederacy? No, that was just his tired brain, he decided. Finally, Turner looked up. His eyes were deeply set by the lack of sleep. "Sir, I'm not entirely sure where to start." That was certainly true.

That was not what the man wanted to hear, and while he did not move, his eyes lit up with a look that said he was unafraid to use violent means to get what he wanted.

Clum cleared his throat and scooted his chair slightly between the two men. "Let's be civilized here. John Horton Slaughter, standing in for our town marshal; Thomas Turner ... uh ... sailor, didn't you say?"

"... traveler. That'll work. And not always travelling where I want to go or why." Turner looked up at Slaughter. "Slaughter?"

"Um huh," was all the man replied.

"Truthfully?"

"Um huh."

"Standing in for a town marshal?"

"Lost a bet."

"Do that often?"

Slaughter rolled his eyes and sat back. "Never lost a hand or a round yourself?"

"My father was not a betting man and insisted the same for me.

"Keep it that way. Now answer the question: who dumped you down that mineshaft?"

Taking a deep breath and settling back in his chair, Turner looked Slaughter in the eyes. Yes, this was a former soldier. Just what this town needed: someone who might not have a problem with a New Confederacy. "There are some folks that don't like Northerners. There seem to be quite a number of those around here."

"Guess they don't know the war is over."

Turner was not yet ready to understand him. "Some might even want to start the war again." Slaughter was Southern, but how much did that matter now? Was it possible to believe he might be an ally?

The pause in the conversation was long and for a moment, Clum was afraid for both men. Slaughter didn't take being sassed or challenged, but the stranger had an old grudge it sounded like. It was obvious to a newsman trained to observe. Did Slaughter see this?

Yup. "I ain't got a beef with anything that happened so long ago. Mr. Turner, I am a rancher and sometimes lawman, though never on purpose. I have a ranch here in the Arizona Territory and I would like to see it situated in the State of Arizona. I'm a practical man, and don't go in for nostalgia. No use livin' in the past." He nodded toward Turner. "That scar speaks volumes to me. Thought you might be some sort of villain, come here to do your trouble. But I'm bettin' that you're a survivor." He waited, ignoring the alarm in Clum's face. "Belle Isle? Libby? Andersonville?"

Turner reluctantly agreed to the third choice.

"I ain't got the words. I can tell you, you ain't got an enemy here if you ain't up to no good. The question is … what are you up to? Why don't I want to keep you locked up here until the real marshal returns?"

"The less you know, the better. There are things out there chasing me that make a bunch of bandits look like Sunday School children."

"Don't play with me boy."

"Mister, I've been held and tortured by people who want to own the world, or at least a large piece of it. They're building machines of war and getting ready to attack. That's all I'm going to say to a civilian." He wasn't trying to sound rude and he hoped that both Clum and Slaughter understood he wasn't being facetious.

The Tombstone men looked at one another, confused.

Slaughter screwed up his face. "Are you insane?"

"Quite possibly. I'm tired and hurting. And I'm done with being chased. I want peace and quiet myself. I never intended to drag anyone into this. It's my own cross. Will you allow me to keep my secrets on the promise that knowledge, this time, comes at too dear a price?" He rested his head in his hands. "I admire that you chose not to live in the past, sir. Wiser than me."

Slaughter sat back in his chair, glancing up at Clum once before speaking. "Some men can't escape it. Peace ain't for them. But maybe … maybe we can get it for the others. Maybe that's what we're here for."

Clum was rather surprised by the philosophical admission Slaughter offered. He'd known the man for a few years, not many, but he'd always seemed to be quietly keeping to himself unless provoked.

"Whatever is following you, it can't be worse than your past. Trust me on that." Slaughter sat up. "Forward's where you're going, boy. Stop looking back. And I say that from experience. Now … I'm making my choice. I want you to tell me everything. I have a sneaking suspicion I know what you're gonna say. Been hearing things myself. Don't like what I'm hearing. I'll have the whole truth from you if you please." It was not a request.

Turner realized he hadn't said anything for a few minutes and looked up. "How did you end up a temporary town marshal?"

"As I said, I lost a bet. It's temporary, just as you say."

Clum piped in, "We're running him for Cochise County Sheriff."

Slaughter shook his head, recalling some of his friends and family who were still caught up in a war that had ended two decades before … caught up like Turner. "Sheriff? Never happen."

It wasn't the Palace Hotel by a long shot, but it had a roof and a door that could be locked – or more importantly, unlocked. It wasn't the marshal's jail cell. It was a miracle and a kindness that Clum vouched for him. John Clum, as owner of the *Epitaph* along with being the one-time town Mayor, and who knew what else, had often slept on the premises, waiting for important news from the outside world to arrive by telegraph. Tombstone had neither the consequence nor the population base to warrant visits from international journalists nor even the Reuters Heavy Haulers – carriers of bulk cargo and the latest reports. Though the Earp incident had drawn the most squalid interest, it didn't last, leaving the sleepy mining town to fend for itself with a rail line nearby and a telegraph. With all the violence in the whole world, events at the OK Corral faded quickly.

The office was quiet and cold. A smell of ink and hot paper lingered in the air. During the day, Turner could imagine the chaos that he assumed came with the printing of a newspaper. In the evening, Clum must have found things as Turner was finding them – peaceful. Not quite as peaceful as that moment in the desert, but enough so.

Yet, events of the past couple of years must had left Clum a little paranoid and thus he promised that the backroom was secure enough for Turner's satisfaction, and was locked at all times. Only he, and now Turner, had the key.

Except … The door was slightly ajar, allowing light into the room.

No such thing as security.

Someone was in the room.

Turner set down the bag with some small goods he'd acquired and the key he should have been obligated to use … quietly. There was a chance that the intruder was not after him, instead was lying in wait for Clum. The editor and owner of the *Tombstone Epitaph* newspaper had been forced to put his business up for sale and to surrender any aspirations for his town by a faction of Democratic sympathizers. All were former Southern soldiers and conservatives. They gladly employed thugs, who were called *Cowboys* despite the term being derogatory. Likely a joke amongst them.

In light of all that Clum had done for him, Turner was feeling considerably protective of the man. If this was a Cowboy sent to terrorize Clum, the villain was in for a nasty surprise. A small pistol of Clum's was just inside his pocket and Turner was careful in removing it. No sound. Smooth. Silent.

He crossed the room, carefully balancing his weight on each foot, preparing to react should the wooden floorboards creak.

A small sound drifted out to him. The turning of a page?

Turner's hand rested on the door, and with an empowering deep breath, he shoved his way in.

A figure of a man sat on the bed, looking more than a little startled. There was enough light for him to read but not enough to show any distinguishing features to Turner. Slowly, the man set down his book, raised his hands in submission, and stood up. "Monsieur, please do not shoot me."

Backing out into the main office, Turner reached over to the lamp and turned it up. The man by the bed was impeccably dressed, by his speech a Frenchman, and more than disturbed by the immediate circumstance.

"Monsieur. My English is acceptable but not excellent. Do you understand? Should I speak Spanish?"

"English is fine. Who are you?"

"Please call me ... uh ... Gabriel. I'm not very angelic, no?" He began to lower his hands, when a gesture from Turner scared him into raising them again. "I cannot hurt you."

Narrowed eyes were the only response Turner was going to give him.

"Monsieur, I am here to meet someone."

"Who?"

"One Monsieur Turner, who I now suspect is you? Oui. It is. Please Monsieur Turner, I'm over fifty years old and my circulation does not permit me to stand like this for very long."

"Fine. Sit down there and don't do anything stupid."

"That may be impossible, Monsieur. I am too human and cannot avoid foolish or idiotic moments. But if I may, I will sit here very still." Gabriel folded his hands neatly and waited for Turner to review each corner of the room until he was satisfied that Gabriel was alone.

Turning to the French man, not taking the courtesy of pointing his gun elsewhere, Turner put one foot up on a crate and leaned on his leg. "French? You were sent by Hetzel. How are *you* planning on trying to kill me?"

Gabriel looked offended for a moment, then thought and replied, "I am not here to kill you, nor to capture you, nor to cause you any grief. I am here because all other efforts to communicate with you have met with disaster – most often caused by the messenger rather than the recipient."

"Are you telling me, Mr. Gabriel ... which is likely not your name ... that you are not enhanced?"

"Neither enhanced nor improved. Just as my mother bore me."

"But you were sent by Hetzel?"

"May I explain?"

Turner pushed himself back and leaned against the wall. "I surely wish you would."

"Not using my own name is of use both to you and to me. If you should decide to trust me, and if I feel you will not be endangered ... and neither will I ... then I'll tell you my real name. As for my message, I am here to share with you a plan I think you will like – and the last communication one hopes from Monsieur Hetzel. A plan devised by Monsieur Hetzel and myself ... yes, me ... that will satisfy him that you are no longer a threat. And, as such, you may go on with your life. I am not mechanically ... what is another word ... ah, yes, augmented. If I were to wrestle with you here and now, I would lose. I am fit," he said patting himself on the chest, "but a bit worn by age." The man smiled a little. His eyes squinted when he grinned, his cheeks pushing their flesh upward. A trim white beard filled the lower half of his face. He was neither tall nor short, and as average in his build. By the tan skin of his hands, he clearly spent time outdoors.

For a moment Turner thought about all that had happened. "I've heard that same story before. Last message? Best offer? Then they tried to kill me anyway."

107

"Who did?"

"Your Egyptian."

"Not mine," Gabriel muttered in anger. "The Egyptian, Monsieur Cairo, was recalled to Paris, but it would seem he is no longer obeying orders. Yes. I cannot say I am sorry enough. He was never to have made such a violent attempt on your life, unless of course my information is wrong, which is entirely possible. I am only a writer and not particularly privy to all of Monsieur Hetzel's dealings. All I know is that I have been assured that mine is the last communication, and it is one of peace. I am not armed."

Turner waited, trying to digest what he was hearing. "Cairo intimated threats against a civilian of my acquaintance." He couldn't bring himself to use her name, in case she was not the object of Hetzel's machinations.

"You mean Dr. Gantry? I was assured that she has come to no harm. Please … I promise you. I, myself, would never acquiesce to a woman being subjected to this mad world of intrigue. I have Monsieur Hetzel's word on the matter."

Scoffing, Turner pulled over a chair and sat down. "People can lie."

"Oui. They most certainly can. I am not naïve – and I believe Monsieur Hetzel."

Turner stared at him for a moment. The thought that anyone would even dare mention Lettie in the same breath as Hetzel made his heart pound. "You want my trust? Then answer me this much." As Gabriel seemed to be excited by the prospect, Turner continued. "Is Captain Robur alive? Does Hetzel have him. The Egyptian said he was alive and … enhanced."

Gabriel's eyes grew sad. "That is of great value to you? Of course. Monsieur Turner, you are living up to your reputation, even amongst your enemies. I would have thought having learned what he did to you that you would not care whatever happened to him. But you do." He sat looking at the floor for a long time. "It is refreshing," he said with half a voice. "I have been involved in so much nonsense that a little natural loyalty and compassion are a surprise." He took a long breath and raised his head. "Do not pity me, I am well employed, serve my country, and am able to follow my passion for storytelling. Which is what you and I will do. We will tell a story that diverts attention from the true story of Captain Robur and will encourage others to leave you alone."

"You didn't answer my question."

"I swear that I know what you know: Captain Robur died in the East Indies last year. That Cairo told you otherwise seems to me to be yet another act of cruelty. He can be that way. I am not fond of him. Too petty."

Turner lowered his gun. "I need a drink." He hadn't considered it before, but his shoulders and chest felt lighter, even if his heart was hammering. He couldn't stand the idea of Robur being made into one of Hetzel's army. A wave of pity and futility washed over him and he found he'd been sitting for a long time, silent. Gabriel was watching him, patiently. The expression of terror the Frenchman had originally had now altered to one of commiseration. "Cairo? Petty? That sounds just about right. He's not on your side anymore; you do realize that, yes? Not just off orders, he is actively working for your enemy, the Prussians."

Gabriel was taken aback by the suggestion. "I thought Cairo was simply being disobedient, perhaps in a foolish attempt to win back favor from Monsieur Hetzel."

"He's joined up with a New Confederacy and Prussian agents. A woman and a giant."

"Mon dieu. That will not please Monsieur Hetzel. France and Prussia have not forgiven the other after the war of 1871. Unification with the German states did nothing to distract the Kaiser from his revenge. I can't say that I recall anything of that conflict with pleasure." He stood up, watching to see if Turner would react defensively. "If you are amenable, we may need to discuss your insight into this traitor. I would not like to think what might happen due to one of Monsieur Hetzel's agents associating with Prussia."

"Don't you think Hetzel has considered this? Surely he can't control every one of his monsters and those who know of them. He must have a plan for such an emergency."

Gabriel looked as though someone had struck him. "Of course. But I cannot say what those plans are. I am not privy to such things …"

"You're just a writer."

He nodded in response to Turner's comment. "If you will permit me, I wish to send a telegram, to my employer. The sooner I tell him we are in contact, the sooner he will feel greater confidence in our plan."

Turner raised an eyebrow. "You'll end up showing him where we are."

"That can be hidden. And if you allow me this, I believe I will be able to achieve some peace of mind for you. In the meantime, Monsieur, if I may, I think I should like to join you in that drink."

As entertainment went, Gabriel was used to some of Paris's more interesting ideas of what constituted "theater." The Oriental met none of those ideas. There was an opulence to the place; contrived and mis-sized. The room was quite small and shaped like the letter "L." To the left stretched a long, ornate bar of dark oak. Behind the barkeeper stood a mirror framed by three arches decorated with columns. The wall paper was cluttered but not fading. Clearly the owners desired a polished look but it seemed so out of place in the Arizona desert. Faro tables presented a line along the windows, seating the dealer with his back to the congestion along Allen Street. An occasional clomping of boots and jangling of oversized, decorative but useless spurs accompanied the shadows that streaked across the glass panes. The rest of the facility provided seating for drinks and occasional games of chance. Toward the far end, a piano player provided music to fill in the time between sets played by a small band. There might be a singer later on, Turner and Gabriel were told, but no one could confirm it.

The Oriental tried its best to be modern and tony. It wanted a higher class of player to come in and leave most of his money, preferably without shooting or destroying the furniture.

Several private games were in play … surprisingly friendly and humorous: the direct opposite of what all the dime novels said of the wild frontier. A pair of "Hostesses" lingered near the bartender. Were it not for the gaudy colors they wore, one might not have picked them out of a crowd of average townswomen. One was dressed particularly nicely which meant that she was either a part owner in the establishment or one of the more expensive "doves." She might well just be a Hostess with no duties behind the scenes, but to the righteous folk in town there was little to no difference.

The better dressed woman smiled and watched as Gabriel sauntered up to the bar.

Why yes, it turned out that they had wine – French wine, no less. Gabriel was elated and, Turner noted with amusement, clearly aware how his being a Parisian was exotic enough to gain him a few advantages. The service improved and it took no time for the Hostesses to approach.

Turner was a rather handsome fellow, but tonight was Gabriel's evening.

"Shall I get you a room at the Grand Hotel, Monsieur?" he said, returning with two glasses.

"I'm fine with my accommodations."

"No. We must arrange better for you. Remember, I sat on that bed ... you will not be comfortable. Allow me one small gesture here. Besides," he added, sipping his wine, "it will be at my employer's expense."

There was a shout from one of the Faro tables. Turner played with his glass but did not drink. "What does your employer want?"

"Straight to the point! Oui. Monsieur Hetzel, and I, for I do not want you to think I have no ... um ... stake in this matter. We will use a publication to tell the story of Jean Robur and the magnificent airship, the *Albatross*. I will adjust certain details to distract and redirect individuals who might want to learn more. I have done this before. Successfully. But I must understand the details. It must be believable. Do you understand what I am proposing?"

"I believe I do," and Turner added with a lopsided smile, "Mr. Gabriel."

"This is not so easy a task, but that too many easily believe what they hear or read, and take as fact anything in print, makes it a possible task. One might label something as fiction a hundred times and there will always be those who readily accept or criticize you for what was published as though it were the truth." Gabriel shook his head.

"And, if I am understanding you correctly, my role will be minimalized."

Gabriel leaned in conspiratorially. "I was thinking of making you a short, stout, English fellow. Could you be comfortable with that? Just think. If you were no longer *that* Thomas Turner, why Monsieur, you could become whomever you wish to become. If *that* Thomas Turner disappeared into the jungle or ocean, along with

Captain Robur, then the living man here and now could not possibly be him."

"It's all too clever for me, Mr. Gabriel. While I suspect I really have no choice ..." He paused as two cowboys staggered past their table, jostling it slightly. A moment passed when everyone was waiting to see if a fight might break out over the disrespectful slight. Turner only nodded at the men and went back to his conversation – to the relief of everyone. "I suspect I will need to go along with this convoluted plan, but will you allow me an evening to think it through."

"Of course, Monsieur. Besides, I believe I owe you something I have promised."

To his shock, Gabriel suddenly found himself too interesting to a pair of working girls who had sidled up to him and were being quite inappropriate in their behavior. Gabriel was reasonably shocked that any female might behave that way, but was too much of a gentleman to insult them by sending them away.

Turner tried not to laugh. Like Gabriel, he was a man raised to behave as a gentleman, and despite the lack of funds to support a gentle lifestyle, he genuinely wanted to be perceived as one. He couldn't help it. As one of the girls ran her fingers through Gabriel's white hair and attempted the worst French he'd ever heard, the poor Frenchman looked to Turner who could only laugh out loud. He did his best to disentangle his new companion.

She sat in her parlor, staring at the message.

At once she wanted to dance, to cry, to scream ... instead, she did what her mother taught her: she sat calmly in a ladylike fashion. Looking up at the messenger, with his smart cap and polished shoes, she knew she could show no emotion.

"Young man, if you would wait a moment, I should like to give you a response for immediate transmission." It's a shame, she thought, that the Tipsy didn't go that far. The Transatlantic Pneumatic System only sent real letters and small items to the eastern coast of America, but no further. This response required urgent delivery.

On her desk, which had become a jumbled mess of books and diagrams, rock samples and revised official presentations, she found a pencil and a blank sheet of paper.

The received message read:

Yankee alive. Must know of your condition. Reply paramount.

The name of the person who sent it and that it came from the American frontier surprised her. It was so improbable that she simply had to believe the request was genuine. Telegrams were expensive still and she wrote down the few words she could reliably expect to be understood.

For a moment she hesitated handing back the reply. "Another moment, if you please." She pulled a second piece of paper out of her drawer and wrote the entirety of the situation to Mr. Holmes of Baker Street. It was only right that she keep him informed of what she learned and any actions taken.

Finally Lettie folded the note to Holmes and slid it into an envelope. Handing the messenger the two correspondences, she said, "One is for urgent reply to the telegram. The other is for immediate delivery by hand."

He tugged on his cap and walked out to the hallway with the maid, who paid him for his services from a coin purse near the door.

In the parlor, which was little more than a working scientist's office in actual usage, Lettie sat down by the window and watched as the messenger darted out into the rain, her precious words tucked into his coat pocket. It was raining. Hard. Each drop hit the window, carried into the glass by a steady bluster. The trees were little more than skeletons waving in the wind. She pressed her fingers to the window as the young man disappeared into the haze of rain, fog, and cold.

A pistol fired twice into the air and drunkard mishandling it was supremely pleased that he'd managed to hit the ceiling … once.

Turner was surprised when Gabriel didn't react more than a slight flinch. His amazement must have shown on his face for Gabriel smiled at him, his white whiskers turning upward. "Ah, oui. You must suspect that a man my age would have lived through the bombing of Paris by the Prussians. From balloons. I think this is the point in history when warfare became the purview of mad scientists."

Shaking his head, Turner replied over the rim of his glass, "we saw things here, during the War of the Rebellion, that would convince you otherwise. Machines – crude but often too effective. Walking monstrosities."

"So I have heard," Gabriel said, finally being surprised by the contents of his glass. Wine, it was not. "I am glad that such things have been abandoned." By the tone of his voice, he clearly knew that he was being somewhat insincere if not outright hypocritical. Yet, he was speaking aloud in a crowded room. As if to emphasize his point, Gabriel placed one hand on his heart and swallowed down the remains of the glass, which was causing him a bit of fuzziness. Pleasant fuzziness.

Turner decided that an evening of entertainment and relaxation was not the time to argue Gabriel's point. Beyond Hetzel's bio-mechanical creatures, there were plenty of men out there willing to build monsters driven by steam pressure and hydraulic fluids. He indicated Gabriel's drink with his. "*That*, I am assured, is the 'good stuff.'" For a moment, he let the harsh liquid descend into his stomach, something he knew he'd regret later but frankly didn't care at the moment. How funny that Gabriel was unaware of what his employer had in his arsenal. Turner really felt Gabriel would be horrified to learn of the scorpion-like machine Hetzel sent after him in Hawaii. He liked Gabriel. And, he believed it was unlikely that the man knew the full extent of Hetzel's operations. For that matter,

Turner wasn't fully aware and if the offer of peace was genuine, it might be wise for him to accept it.

A fellow wearing a shirt, trousers, billed cap, and arm garters walked into the theater, as though nothing going on bothered him. He was looking for someone. Spying Gabriel, he walked directly over to the Frenchman, whispered something, and handed over a telegram.

Gabriel read the note, grinned and handed it to Turner.

Slowly Turner opened the folded telegram. The message was simple.

In excellent health. Relieved to hear of Yankee. Hope he read my letter. Signed, L. G.

"I owe you, Mr. Gabriel." He could say nothing more. He could think nothing more. Yet, he could believe it was from her. Who else knew of the letter? He had to remain calm. No one should ever know of his interest in the lady and those who did know should never see confirmation of that knowledge. With everything going on in the room and the potential of a new future, he could push her out of his mind. Somewhat ...

The older man said nothing as he sipped at the brown drink, but his expression remained vastly amused.

A woman, well past her bloom yet striking and unconcerned about age or beauty, strolled confidently to the center of the tiny stage. "Boys, if ya want to hear me sing, put 'em away."

The childish, grumbling groan from much of the crown said the choice between being entertained and shooting the place up had been a strenuous one.

Turner watched while sufficient time was provided to get everyone settled. The Bird Cage had become so much a part of the McLaury – Earp scandal that was less than three years old. The irony was that the Elite Theater was renamed the Bird Cage the year following the legendary shoot out between the brothers and the Cowboys, yet it was identified by the New York Times as not only a place of legend but the "wildest, wickedest night spot between Basin Street and the Barbary Coast." Such little details are often lost, he thought. Turner had noted the year 1881 prominently displayed on the front of the building, and since it was a topic few had stopped talking about, he understood that the gunfight had occurred a couple months prior to the theater's opening. It was a physical impossibility that the feud had been played out in that location. No one really seemed to care. It was Tombstone, and the general consensus was that if it was Tombstone, it was part of the legend being grown by a variety of dime novelists and journalists who'd never set foot outside of St. Louis.

A strong, friendly had clamped down on Turner's shoulder. John Clum quickly offered his salutations before sitting down. He also readily accepted Turner's requirement for a stiff drink. Clum was there to join him and to buy him another if needed – and it would be. "For the record, Mr. Turner, you've been denied a room at the Grand."

"I don't quite fit their requirements – can't say I blame them." Quietly, he slipped the telegram into his coat pocket.

"Nonsense," Gabriel interjected. "I shall complain to the manager. "

Turner took another deep drink. "Their establishment …"

"Oui! Yet, I will insist … a hotel whose reputation may be sullied by complaint."

Clum and Turner looked at each other, drank, then began laughing. "Monsieur," Clum chuckled, "I suspect you would not survive long here in Tombstone. But I like your fuss."

Turner liked his loyalty. "To complaint!" He raised his glass and began to recognize the first signs that the alcohol might be taking effect. "Wait, we're missing someone. Where's old Texas John?"

"Shush. Never call him that."

"He was a Texas Ranger, wasn't he? He's known as Texas John Slaughter."

"Yes, but he's a man with a reputation he doesn't want sullied by a fancy moniker. Men like that find themselves facing off with other men with sillier nicknames."

Nodding, Turner couldn't disagree. "So, where is Mr. Slaughter?"

Gabriel nearly dropped his glass. "Slaughter? His name is Slaughter? He didn't make that up?"

"Ironic," Turner said. God, how he loved irony in life. It was better than any comedy ever produced, and real.

Clum leaned back in his chair and pointed to the far side of the building, in an alcove under the balcony seating. "He's over there – losing more money."

The diminutive man was deeply embroiled in a card game. The nature of his hand was not to be discovered by any expression on his face. Cold. Sharp. Focused. According to Clum, the chances were not in his favor, certainly not lately. If he lost, he'd have to face the only person in all of Arizona and Mexico who was unafraid of him: Mrs. Slaughter.

As the entertainment for the evening was starting up, Turner noticed how small the place was, in fact, how small everything was. Legend had enlarged every detail, as legends are wont to do. He had expected so much more. The newspapers and novels were brimming with descriptions of the great mining metropolis and the vast desert surrounding it. Well, the land *was* wide and mostly empty of human habitation. The rest ... it was decidedly reduced. Though in fairness, it was economically sized. Lumber, food, and goods were all shipped in, and one made the best of what they had through thrift.

The stage only took up half the width of the building, sitting squarely between two private viewing boxes, called "cribs," with their red velvet curtains and padded chairs facing the performance area. A door lead under the stage, probably to the actor's dressing rooms and storage. Wide steps, on the left, lead to the backstage, and a few other places of business. A piano nestled up against the right-hand crib on the floor beneath the stage. Benches were lined up down the open room for those with common tickets. If a man had more cash, he might purchase a table such as the one Turner was seated at, or he might hire out one of the second story boxes lining both sides of the hall.

Like the Oriental, it was surprisingly clean, especially for a mining town in the middle of the desert. Of course, Tombstone wanted a better reputation, more than what the novels gave it, yet with the silver almost gone it seemed that soon it would fade into a memory of mythological men and sudden death.

As the singer started into her known routine, many of the audience joining in the songs, Turner caught himself comparing her to Lettie Gantry. Oh, how he wasn't going to think of Lettie. Besides, it wasn't fair. Thoughtfully, he reached up to his breast and touched the leather pouch he'd saved from the train. Where the singer had the look of a woman fading, perhaps due to the harsh living conditions, Lettie seemed unable to age. This was likely his imagination at work, especially under the circumstances; he'd only known Dr. Lettie Gantry a little over a year. She had been the focus of his intense study – how else could he have caught her. He smiled; truth be told, she'd outsmarted him and it was he who was captured. In the end, she'd even gone so far as to forgive him his trespasses and sent him home. Perhaps it would be impossible for such a woman to lose her brilliance in his memory. He would never see her as aged. The one or two gray hairs in her shiny black hair seemed unusual and out of place for her, yet honestly they were there. He might have put them there with the appalling way he'd originally treated her. She'd never lost her bloom because she'd lived a life full of passion in the pursuit of her dreams. *In excellent health*; indeed she was. She was a lady; a fine, well-bred, intelligent lady. Her soft voice, with that proper pronunciation, made everything sound pleasant. Her green eyes never missed a thing but her gentleness often kept her amused thoughts to herself. Dear God, he was relieved to know she was alive.

"You have the look of a man who is in love, Monsieur Turner."

Turner lifted his drink to his lips, partially to conceal that "look." He waited, unsure how to answer without saying her name. "Love" had not been a word he'd considered before. It would be foolish of him to expend an emotion so important on a woman who would not have him and was wise enough to have made that decision. Love? Could he love someone? Could he be loved in turn?

"You need not reply. Your eyes tell the whole story."

Clum kept glancing back and forth, confused and curious. So, there really was more to Tom Turner than he'd discovered. Good. He'd quiz Gabriel about it later. He was a newsman after all.

Before Clum could say a word, pithy or otherwise, their table began to quiver, then shake.

All the tables were shaking. Not a hard shake, but enough to be noticed.

Silence fell over the room as everyone looked to see if the glasses next to them were registering the vibrations.

They were.

"Collapse!" one man shouted.

Turner stared, eyes wide, at Clum for an answer as the room continued to vibrate.

"This whole place is built on caverns and mines. But ... but this doesn't feel like ..." Clum stood up. The audience was beginning to panic. There had been so much drinking that few were of a clear enough mind to know what to do. "Everyone!" Clum shouted, surprised that he actually garnered any immediate attention. He cleared his throat and used that voice which must have made his mayoral campaign speeches effective. "Take up your beverages, gentlemen, and head outside. Pay attention to the ground and keep clear of the buildings for a while."

There seemed to be a general lack of argument and quickly the room emptied. Several unpurchased bottles left with the crowd, but even the bartender wasn't concerned as much as he was determined to get outside himself.

The shaking stopped. Turner commented that it seemed more like a rattle; was that truly what a mine collapse would feel like? In two overly simplified sentences he described the earthquakes in the East Indies before Krakatoa erupted. The immediate situation was dire enough that the newsman Clum didn't think to ask more questions on such a potential story.

"The chandelier isn't moving that much. If this was an earthquake, that thing would be swinging wildly." Turner pointed up to the bullet-riddled ceiling.

"It may be a blessing – a collapse would be a disaster." Clum redirected one man headed away from the door and toward the bar.

"It's stopped," the man protested.

"Out!"

Gabriel waited patiently. This was not in his experiences. "Forgive me, but are you saying this town is built on mine shafts? Open holes in the ground?"

Clum nodded reluctantly. "People just kept digging until they'd tunneled under here. And in some places, they just kept building until they covered something abandoned. I don't think anyone really put too much thought in it. We need to go, Monsieur."

April 1884
Outside the Bird Cage on Allen Street
Tombstone, Arizona Territory

Turner, Gabriel and Clum were the last men out ...

... and the first ones to see it.

At the edge of town, lit by the pale ineffectiveness of two gas-burning street lamps, a great black creature waited in a mist. A creature or something. Ghostly. Demonic. It could barely be seen.

"What kinda beast is that?" Clum sputtered.

It was breathing. Hissing. Swirls of mist drifted around it.

Popping noises. Metal expanding.

God Almighty, Turner thought. "It's a machine."

"A what?"

"That, gentlemen, is a locomotive built for the Devil himself." With the suggestion made, it was easier to see the vague outline of a train. The round boiler, a short smoke stack, the pilot catch. There was more. Something in the shape suggested that there were protrusions out each side near the wheels. With the steam catching light and obscuring the engine in a white veil, it looked like an angry ghost. Turner knew that ghost.

Gabriel took one step forward but no more. "Not of ours," he said quickly.

"I know," Turner whispered back.

Clum turned to them. "There's no track here. How the hell ..."

The giant black engine turned on its headlamp, flooding Allen Street in a blinding white light. The chemical burned off its initial brilliance and drew back into an eerie, intense orange glow. It was effective: a man at the far end of the street could have read his watch by it.

In the new light, they could no longer make out anything of the engine's shape and no features that the light didn't strike. Turner finally had to hold his hand out in front of his eyes.

The ghost engine shot out a blast of steam on either side and began forward. There was excessive rumbling and shaking. The machine was the cause; not a mine collapse. As it moved forward Clum kept yelling that this was impossible – there was no track. Horses pulled loose from hitching posts and scattered, making Allen Street a stampede zone.

The machine took up most of the street. Its height matched the tallest store front. Whatever steered it was not precise, and it clipped the corner of 4th and Allen streets, knocking out the front support columns on the Oriental. Screams followed a crack of wood and a crash of material as the second story balcony collapsed to the ground, blockading the Oriental's front entrance. Men and women fled back into the upper rooms and out the back exits. A wagon was crushed as the thing steered back to the center of the street.

The ghost kept coming, unhindered by anything. More steam blasted out from its sides and the crowds panicked. Two hapless miners were caught in the blistering steam jets.

"Monsieur, get inside!" Turner commanded.

"You think it can't be stopped?"

"It can. It has a boiler, metal, fuel, and an engineer. It's humanly designed and it can be stopped. Please get inside!"

Gabriel looked offended. "I will not! This is not a mechanism of France or America. I know its look – I have seen it – this is Prussian. I will not flee from them. I did not in '71 and I shall not now."

"You're unarmed," Clum chimed in, while drawing a small pistol from his coat pocket. What good it would do, he wasn't certain. But he would not be unprepared.

Gabriel nearly scoffed but in good form chose not to make his doubt known. "I am armed with science, sir. We should, as you say, fight this fire with fire, here and now."

Turner shook his head vigorously, understanding the satisfying yet futile comfort Clum found in his gun. "There's not enough time. We need to find its Achilles Heel. I've been on her and she isn't like anything we know."

At this, Clum glared at Turner. "You know this thing? Why didn't you tell us?"

"I did. It's the same locomotive we all believed was already down in Mexico."

"There are no rails here!"

Gabriel put his hand on Clum's shoulder and the three men began backing away from the relentlessly moving machine quickly. "It has its own rails, do you not see, there."

He was pointing correctly at the strange protrusions on either side of the wheel base. As Turner knew, the wheels were outrageously sized, but here they lay underneath a sheath of riveted iron, wider than two human bodies. From under the edge, it was easily seen that the locomotive no longer relied on narrow wheels on rail, but on a wide track of rubber and metal ties; grouped in four sets of three wheels, making the monstrosity – in railroad terms – an impossible 4-6-6-0-6-6-4. The arm of each piston was connected by an articulated ball to a shaft linking the wheels in the set. An impossible design, yet there it was. The thing had brought its own rails in the form of Dreadnaught Wheels. Their width kept it from sinking in the sandy soil of the Arizona Territory, like a camel in the Sahara.

To Turner's mind, it was worse than the dirigible *Albemarle II*. If this thing could turn its treaded wheel groupings independently, it could not only go forward and backward, but could steer with limited control. He kept backing away, sometimes nearly falling as he stumbled on chairs or warped boards in the walkway. Gabriel stayed close to him out of morbid curiosity, and Clum clearly had decided his pistol was all that was keeping the three of them alive.

The ghost engine rolled forward.

"See how it moves, Monsieur Turner. If they can progress only one side at a time, here too they can sharply turn. This is a dreadful innovation, which one neither of us should be surprised by, oui?"

"Yes. Oui." He stopped. "It's still operated by a man. We can stop this if we eliminate the engineer." Turner began moving forward. Yes, he was not surprised they'd developed the contraption so far. No fear. This was a human invention not a ghost or monster. The more he recalled his stay onboard the train, the angrier he became, and he used that anger to propel him forward. Foolishly, he walked out in front of the thing and stood, defiantly.

Slowly, it stopped. If it could have laughed, it would have.

"Mister, get out of its way!" John Slaughter was suitably sober, furious, and armed. Restraining himself from comment about the puny size of Clum's gun, he simply offered a rifle in an extended hand. Clum, not a fool, gladly took it. Nothing was offered to

Gabriel, which suited the Frenchman just fine. He was taking every chance to get closer; to examine the vehicle's mechanisms.

"No sir! This thing goes no further. It's a goddamned machine and we can stop it!"

Turner had not moved from his place which irritated Slaughter to no end. Still, if he had to say, it was a brave stance to take. He understood brave but stupid or impossible stances. In only a heartbeat's time, he was standing next to Turner.

A long hiss from the locomotive was followed by the sound of men ... many men ... coming out of the train. As they emerged from the mist on either side of the machine, it was clear that the crew had expanded over the last days to include local cowboys and bums. Slaughter counted automatically – a survival skill he never failed to engage. Twelve. Eight on the left. Four on the right. Armed with pistols. One had a rifle – new – probably a large caliber. Slaughter muttered this to Turner who was impressed, until the situation snatched his attention back.

From the left-hand side, the group of men parted to allow a looming figure to walk through them, with a smaller man immediately behind. The little man blotted his forehead; the larger man folded his arms across his chest. Deichgraef.

"That's a big son of a bitch."

"As vile and nasty as he looks," Turner replied. "The little fellow isn't much different."

"This is going to get ugly. No one comes to a fight with a gun unless he plans to use it. Those are old hands. Some may be former soldiers. They're used to bullying their way but the most effective bully commits at least one act of violence to prove himself. They don't know you – do they?"

"The big man does. The others I don't remember seeing."

The lack of fearful response from the two men in front of their huge locomotive was starting to draw comment amongst the cowboys.

"Cowboys. An' that ain't a compliment. Rustlers, thieves, whoring bums."

"Not the type to abide by Marquess of Queensbury rules?" Turner didn't mean to sound snide, but he knew the type of man he was facing.

Slaughter didn't speak – he nodded.

Deichgraef stepped forward. "Herr Turner. You look too much alive."

"Disappointed?" Sarcasm … the last weapon of the desperate or the annoyed, Turner thought.

"You must be a sailor who knows how to swim."

"No. I just have better skills than your coffin maker."

"Or better luck, ja?"

"Ja," Turner mimicked him.

Slaughter leaned in to Turner. "You damn well better tell me what this is all about when we're done."

Turner felt the rifle shoved into his hand. How he wished he was as proficient as Lettie Gantry with one of these things, but he was in no position to request a revolver. Oh hell, at least he had more shots than a Colt revolver would give him.

Every one of them were standing no more than ten yards apart. The light was not in his favor, Turner noted, squinting. But he had a better idea of the layout of the town. Dark and shadow would serve him.

"The big German is coming after you, now or later. Don't know how the rest will break up."

"Later. He'll send those boys out to test us and stay back, to see what happens."

They didn't have to wait. Deichgraef snapped his fingers and stood still as the cowboys rushed forward. With a shove from Slaughter, Turner knew which direction he would need to go in. Running left, he headed to the alley that was closest to him. Shadow. He needed shadows.

Slaughter tore right, keeping his muzzle pointed down toward to the Cowboys and the train. Clum gripped Gabriel's arm and yanked him away. If anyone had been foolish enough to remain, they scattered into the alleys and buildings, praying that the structures would protect them from gunfire.

Four shots sped past his head. Too close.

Sucking in every breath of air, Turner sprinted down the alley. It was irregular, full of potholes that tried to trip him. The train's light helped a little but he needed to get to Fremont Street. There would be lights from gas lamps but few of them lined the street and he would have the dark to work in.

Drunks and miners ran across Fremont, knowing that the fight was coming toward them.

The sounds of rifles and handguns rang out from Allen Street. Slaughter and Clum were engaging their combatants. It was time to take on the men behind him.

The shouting, the shooting – it all felt like battles he'd been in, so many years ago. For all he knew, as he situated himself behind several crates to see who would pass his vantage point, any one of those cowboys might have been in those same battles, on the other side.

They called out to one another, limited by the lack of light. Not wise. He counted names that were shouted. Clem, Jack, Phil and Bosey. Adding the man shouting, that made five. There had been eight on his side. Three might be working their way over from Allen on 5th Street, to trap him between them. They could hear as well as he could – they had to know that he wasn't moving.

Three men appeared in the gaslight on the south end of the street. Five behind. But they didn't know where Turner was yet.

He had chambered the first round. This was where he still hesitated if given the time to realize how much he dreaded it: he'd have to kill a man – several in fact – it was war. Picking an enemy off was not dishonorable; it was considered a wise battle tactic. He might have the advantage for the first two shots, but not after that.

Eight men.

Shoot.

Move.

Shoot again.

He lifted the rifle up to his shoulder. The first shot had to count, making the fight seven to one. He couldn't fail. Sighting down the barrel, he chose the most obvious target, standing in the light, chest facing him but looking the other way.

Squeeze the trigger. Never pull.

No more thinking.

The recoil of the .44/40 bullet slammed the rifle butt into his shoulder but the barrel stayed level. A classic, well planned shot.

The cowboy dropped. There was no screaming. No flailing. Instant. Ugly, but fast.

Turner chambered another round without moving the rifle off his shoulder or the sight off his second target.

The second cowboy had turned toward the location of the first shot, in fatal curiosity. The bullet struck him in the chest, below the collar and close to the heart. Considering the target was in motion, it was a lucky shot.

Lucky Tom Turner.

Lucky no more. A barrage of bullets flew into the building next to Turner; into and through the crates he was using for cover. He dropped flat onto the ground then rolled toward the building so that he could see what was behind him. In the style of a sniper, he lay belly down and took aim at anything that might move.

Cowboy three fell.

In the distance he could hear the other fight, but there was no time to worry about Clum or Slaughter … or Gabriel wherever he had gone.

Round four – missed.

Round five found the cowboy named Clem and shattered his kneecap, essentially eliminating him from the fight. The wound might well kill him anyway.

Another hailstorm of bullets fell around him.

A slug hit him in the left arm. Someone had figured out that they needed to shoot down toward the ground to get him.

Turner fired two more shots before he realized he'd been hit. Grazed. His arm still worked, though painfully. They'd scratched meat and not bone.

Reload. He'd have to reload soon. At best he had eleven rounds and he'd fired seven.

Bullets shattered the window above his head, showering bits of glass. They'd given him an easier escape through a store. Turner scrambled to his feet and leapt through the window, cutting his leg above his boot slightly. Damn lucky it wasn't a debilitating cut.

They knew where he'd gone but he could gain more cover inside if needed – if no one else was in there. A mining store. Great, if he needed a shovel …

No. As he approached the front of the store, and looked out the window to see who was still on Allen Street, he saw it. A pile of boxes. One box: the perfect box. The box that said God must be on his side, or at least God was fascinated by inventive battles.

As he reached out for it, a shot ricocheted off the floor near his hand. He dropped back onto his seat and fired. A cowboy was midway through the shattered back window. The first shot went wild but his second landed in the part in the cowboy's hairline. The others had not come through the window yet. Maybe they didn't like the new 3 to 1 odds, or they wouldn't climb over the body of their compatriot to get in. Turner wouldn't count on it.

He seized the box and opened it.

Nitroglycerin. Dynamite. Long, lovely sticks of unstable explosives crammed into paper and armed with a fuse.

Two civilians, by their silhouettes, ran past the window of the mining store. He was so trigger happy he nearly fired at them, but reason prevailed. He needed ammunition. Slaughter would have it but where was the man?

Looking again at the back of the store to see if anyone had braved coming through the window then out the front window, he saw no one. Dear God his arm hurt.

Slowly opening the front door, a crack at first then wider and wider, he looked to Allen Street. Crouching as low as he could, Turner ran down the boardwalk planks to the corner and hid himself from the train's headlamp. Carefully, he leaned sideways and checked for movement on the street.

Three clomps of footsteps came up on his right and it was an almost disastrous half second before he recognized Slaughter. Words were not required. Slaughter held up a box of cartridges. Turner held up a stick of dynamite.

"That's different. How do you plan to use it?"

"Get the whole box under the engine and set it off?"

Slaughter looked dubious, though it might well have been his natural expression. "Think you can get near that machine?" Pushing past Turner to have his own look at the situation, Slaughter saw three men run out from the street one block up and join with four men he didn't recognize. New. And of course, the big German was still there, he muttered to Turner. "Odds aren't good."

Turner only shrugged, which hurt more than he'd expected.

He noted the cut on Slaughter's cheek. Either someone had tried to use a knife on him or had fired a lucky shot. Either way, Turner doubted that the attacker was still a threat – Slaughter wouldn't have left him in that state. Turner handed over his rifle and hoisted the whole box under his arm. He had a match in his pocket; he'd hoped to use it on a cheroot cigar, which he was craving at that moment.

Within two steps he knew he couldn't sprint the distance without being gunned down. Bullets blasted into the ground, one ricocheted into the box, and the rest slammed into the store front. Slaughter ducked down behind a water trough and Turner was quick to join him.

"Lousy protection," Slaughter declared of the trough.

"We need to get something under the engine! Can you hit this box if I can get it under there?"

"If you call it a target, I can hit it. But Mister, I don't see how you can get …" he stopped for another pair of slugs whizzing past his head, "… get that box under the engine."

Slaughter was right. Damn it, he couldn't get near.

Clum dove down next to them, dragging a beleaguered Gabriel with him. "Heard you. But then, maybe they did too. Doesn't matter. If we give you cover, you might be able to make it."

"I can shoot. I'm not that good, but they don't know that," Gabriel offered, disappointed he couldn't resolve the matter scientifically.

Slaughter handed out bullets and gave Turner's rifle to Gabriel. "Turner, you really willing to do this?"

"Got a better plan?"

"Nope."

"Want to do it yourself?"

"Nope."

"Then I'm going." He opened the box and took out three sticks, and set them next to Slaughter. "We may need those."

Before Slaughter could approve or complain, Turner nodded to all three men and darted out toward the ghost engine. A hail of support fire followed him, causing cowboys and Deichgraef to run.

What he heard, he wasn't sure. Gunfire, yes. Shouting, maybe. All he could do or see was the target ahead. Get the box under the pilot truck. That meant getting around the catch. No. That meant getting it anywhere near or under the pilot – or on the platform above.

He could hear his heart and the rush of blood in his ears. He didn't want to hear anything else. With both hands he threw the box. It hit the pilot catch at an odd angle and slid slightly upwards landing on the platform. Turner fell from the exertion and landed in the dirt not far from the train. "Slaughter!"

"Get outta' there!"

"Shoot. Now!"

Slaughter stood up and scored four shots into the box. Nothing.

Nothing? How could nothing happen?

The remaining crew and cowboys scattered into the alley. Some ran from the train. Some ran toward the box, to throw it clear of the machine. Deichgraef snarled something at the cowboys, then headed toward Turner.

Gabriel picked up one of the sticks. "I have a better throw than shot." Standing up, he squared off his stance and pitched the stick toward the train. Desperately, Slaughter and Clum both began firing as rapidly as possible, forcing the cowboys to take cover.

Slaughter took a better aimed shot. While the stick of dynamite was slightly short of the target, it erupted the second the bullet hit it, but otherwise did nothing to the train. Turner was blown down and away from the explosion, rolling almost under the far boardwalk. Deichgraef landed on his back, flinging his arms up to protect his face.

"Throw again!" Slaughter commanded, shoving cartridges into his rifle.

Gabriel waited as two men fired in his direction. Clum and Slaughter laid down the best cover fire they could, with their rifles emptying quickly. The elder man was too determined to miss and this time the single stick fell into the slats of the pilot catch, snagging in place.

"Perfect!" Slaughter fired.

At first, the box went up in a ball of white and yellow flame, seeming to challenge but fail to harm the iron monstrosity it sat on. Turner was on his feet again running. So was everyone else, even Deichgraef.

The boiler and its chemicals exploded, sending out a ball of orange flame and a roiling cloud of gas. The flash of memory that raced across Turner's mind was the pyroclastic flow he'd seen in the Indies. The shockwave of the explosion picked him up and hurled him down the street. Windows shattered. Flammable materials ignited. A cloud of black smoke billowed out and up. Sand and dirt filled the air.

Turner rolled onto his back to see a mass of molten metal and shredded iron slide back to the end of the street on its side.

Well ... that had gone better than hoped. Sort of.

"Goddamn it!" Clum cried out. "We're on fire."

Not that any mining town in the desert had escaped flames over the years, but Tombstone was too new to be burning down this soon. By Clum's reaction, Turner guessed it might have happened once or twice before. Two buildings were engulfed, but that was all. If they could keep the fire from jumping the numbered streets running perpendicular to Allen and Fremont, the damage could be minimal. Slowly, he stood up. There wouldn't be anyone left alive or interested in continuing the gun fight. They'd won ... hadn't they? He would have to help them put out the fires. He'd started it.

"No!" the voice screeched.

Clum turned to see who was standing behind him, shouting. He was out of bullets and matches. Slaughter hadn't heard the fellow and had already charged forward to organize any of the sightseers who had come out to stare at the fire and the remains of the bizarre train. From the higher pitch of the fellow's voice, Clum guessed he was upset that he'd been so ungraciously ignored.

"You. Get up." He had a pistol; Clum was effectively unarmed. "Who are you? Why did you do that? That was such a lovely machine. There was no call for you to do such a destructive thing."

It was Gabriel who spoke. "Monsieur Cairo. This entire situation is not necessary. I have orders for us both, from Monsieur Hetzel …"

"Oh, shut up." Cairo whined. "I do not take orders from a … common writer. You shouldn't be here, it's an insult, you know; Hetzel should not have sent you. I had things perfectly under control. Mr. Turner should have been dead already and you should have stayed back in Paris writing your little biographies of no importance. Propagandist."

Gabriel winced at the title, but said nothing on the matter.

"Mister Turner!" the Egyptian shouted. "Stay right where you are. Or I will be forced to shoot them."

Clum looked back at Turner, who quickly glanced around for Slaughter.

Slaughter was nowhere to be seen in the flurry of actions trying desperately to put out the fires. Looking back at Cairo, Turner held out his hands to show he was unarmed, not that he believed that such a technicality would keep Cairo from shooting him. "Considering the state of your locomotive and that you appear to be alone, maybe we can finally reach an agreement?"

"No." He let the word slide out of his mouth. "That is not equitable. You've destroyed the Confederate train, you have killed off a significant number of my men, and there is a matter of honor here. I will not be defeated by some unemployed, mercenary sailor who," he was getting excited by the opportunity to insult Turner, "who betrayed his country to become a kidnapper and thief." He looked down at Clum. "Why don't you tell him, Mister Turner? Tell him what you used to do for a living."

Clum angrily set his emptied rifle in his lap. "Don't say a word, Turner. Whatever it was, it's none of my business. A lot of men come out here to get away from their mistakes. And I don't want you doing anything he orders you to do."

But Cairo wouldn't be put off. "You don't want to know how he kidnapped a woman and took her to the Indies. Heaven only knows what he did to her. But, because of her continued association with Mister Turner, she will have to be dealt with …" He watched with satisfaction Turner's reaction. "… very harshly. My new employers don't like it when they are not feared. Now you'll be afraid, won't you Turner? Now you will respect what I can do."

"You want me, is that it? Is that all? I'm right here."

"I want you to suffer as I have!"

"For the love of Christ, my being pumped full of poisons and beaten isn't suffering enough for you?"

"Maybe I will kill these men and then see if you have had enough?"

Turner held out his arms. "I'm right here. Take your shot or your chance will be gone. You will not threaten or kill another innocent to get to me."

"Stay away! I will shoot!"

For a long, horrible time, Turner listened. A surge of cold raced through his body. He had no feeling in his hands or feet. His heart raced and only the sound of the fire blazing behind him filled his ears. Cairo could never be allowed to find Lettie. Never allowed to hurt her. Clum. Gabriel. He was so tired of the killing – the war – the battles lost.

Texas John Slaughter took the matter out of his hands.

Who knew where the man had been standing, but now he was to Cairo's left. Nothing stood between the Egyptian and Slaughter's rifle. Clum seized Gabriel and threw him to the ground. Turner rushed forward, unnecessarily.

It was over in three seconds and four rifle shots. The Egyptian was not going to squeal or threaten again. Lying in a heap on the ground, he truly looked pathetic. His ever-present handkerchief fluttered into the dirt.

"Herr Turner? Well played. I did not find him satisfactory at all."

Oh hell.

Clum rolled over to see the Prussian standing in the street. He seized Cairo's gun and threw it to Turner.

Deichgraef walked forward with the fire behind him ... limped forward ... his face cast in shadow. Moisture caught glimmers of color where it coated his face – or was it the color of blood?

"It's over, Mister." Slaughter shouted at the Prussian.

"Do not threaten. This is not your fight though I thank you for eliminating an annoyance."

Strangely, Deichgraef took a strong stance in the middle of the street, holding his revolver very low at his side, and adjusting his position toward Turner.

"What are you about?" Turner half-heartedly asked. He knew.

"I read about these duals in your wretched literature. Jessie James. Doctor Holliday. Wild Buffalo Bill. Is this not how it should end?"

"Those are stories. Fantasies. Nothing ever goes by the book."

Deichgraef smiled – was that a smile? He backed up a few steps, not many.

"Was Madame on the train?" Turner asked, though why he couldn't decide. His eyes were on the Prussian yet for a brief second he could remember her voice, her smell, the sound of taffeta. Would she have risked her life at a battle?

"Long gone. You think she even remembers you? You were nothing to her."

Something about the way she'd looked at him, Turner doubted Deichgraef's assessment.

"Turner?" Slaughter stood next to him, his lips barely moving as he spoke. "I'm not convinced this is a fair fight. But I don't think you can let this go on no more."

Turner said nothing, but tightened his grip on the revolver. To blink would be to invite disaster.

"Your fight," Slaughter declared and asked in the same sentence.

Turner nodded.

"Alright, Yankee. Don't be in a hurry." Slaughter held his sawed off shotgun at the ready, but knew the Prussian was not interested in him. "Clear off people! You have a fire to put out!"

The two men were silent and neither had raised his weapon. Quickly, the town began to give way to the scene.

Standing too close for safety but unwilling to move away, Turner's companion waited. He couldn't move. With two halting breaths, he spoke to the Prussian facing Turner. *"Mein Herr. You do not need to do this. It is not for you to do."* Gabriel's German seemed relatively good.

"Go away, old man."

"This is madness. Your locomotive, your employers are destroyed. You can escape and no one will be the wiser. Go home."

Turner could pick out the language but not every word. He understood the gist.

"That is not possible." Deichgraef said with no emotion, his glare at Turner unbroken.

Gabriel backed away and found Slaughter pulling him further back by the elbow.

Turner understood enough of the conversation. Speed and accuracy: the only things that mattered. If any townsmen were left to watch this, he didn't know or care, so long as they stayed safely away. Yet, there were buzzing sounds around him: people, horses, things. Nothing he would pick out or identify. All he could see was the man approximately fifteen feet away from him, backlit by a raging fire. Colt in hand, right hand, at his side. A Prussian trained officer. Faster? Better aim? More confidence?

It ends here.

"Mein Freund. Do what you must." The Prussian's voice was teasing and arrogant.

Tightly focused, looking for the slightest twitch, Turner didn't hear him. Why was he waiting? Why not shoot and be done with it? He could feel his body rock slightly with every heartbeat. The man was unable to distract him. Slaughter's reminder penetrated his focus, "Don't be in a hurry."

Guns were already un-holstered; someone would be shot.

The feeling of the handle diminished into the smooth crescent of the trigger.

Deichgraef's cheek moved. Slight. Involuntary.

The Prussian fired quickest.

Turner felt as if someone had struck his side with a wooden mallet. Before it started to hurt, he took aim … careful aim … fast but not sloppy. The bullet cut through the Prussian's forehead.

Deichgraef fired once more reflexively.

They stood there.

Deichgraef had fired from a low position, seeking speed by not raising his gun past his hip. Accuracy was sacrificed.

Turner had taken a chance by truly aiming. Suddenly his side burned and all reality rushed into his ears. He grasped his wound and felt warm blood flowing out. His shoulder stung as if sliced by a knife, and then erupted in pain. He knew that Slaughter, Gabriel and Clum had all come to his side.

The Prussian was frozen in his stance but soon fell backwards.

No one touched the foreigners lying on the ground. They rushed forward to see Turner half dragged, half carried into the Bird Cage.

The blur that was time to Turner, swept past him. Whiskey was poured into his mouth; onto his wounds. Bandages and cloth that approached bleached white were removed bright red. Talk. Plenty of people were talking at him. Someone with a bit of authority and a big bag gave orders and prodded at him until Turner fell, swallowed up, unconscious.

Somewhere in his ears he could hear Slaughter. "War's over, boy. You can stop fightin' now."

In certain places of the world, the sky has a unique spaciousness that leaves a man to wonder at his finite size and influence. The Dragoon Mountains, half dressed in white, loomed in the distance. Wind and loose dirt whipped in spirals between the remaining buildings the fire had not leveled. It could have been worse.

His doctor would complain, but Turner really didn't care. The cheroot was sweet and for the moment reminded him that he was alive to enjoy it. The sensation of floating away, transported in light that was different from all the other environments he'd known, carried on a wave of red-tinted sand and broken ore, had come back to him. Welcomed.

He wouldn't be lifting his left shoulder for some time. The stitching was primitive but effective enough. His side would be stiff and pained for a while. Even the throbbing beneath his wounds was nothing. He was nothing. He was everything. Like the wind and the snow.

"Nice to see you standin' up," Clum said, approaching with a clean set of clothes for Turner.

He'd have to speak to Clum someday about the man's habit of interrupting his philosophical moments, Turner thought, and greeted the ex-mayor with a genuine, lopsided grin. To his surprise, a neatly dressed John Slaughter was right behind with a bag of ... something.

"I'm glad to be standing. I want to thank you ..."

Slaughter held his hand up, walked passed him, into the doctor's office, and left the bag next to Turner's few goods. "Some small things are in here. My wife insisted."

"I do thank you sir."

"Ain't needed."

"I believe it is."

"Nope. I like a man who will stand with and for others. You did. So I did."

Few words. That was Slaughter. Clum shook his head and laughed. "You can add these to your collection. They should fit you. Not so much me, anymore," he added, patting his stomach.

"You both…"

"I'll tell you something about us frontier types – we do what we do and don't worry much about thanking anyone. Too much yammerin'."

Slaughter nodded in agreement.

"Well, I can plead ignorance on account that I'm no Western man." Turner offered his hand, recalling how difficult it had been for the scientist, Tesla, to touch another human. Clum and Slaughter had no such difficulties.

Slaughter didn't let go quite as fast. "What are you then? I got a feeling you weren't too sure until now. The territory has a reputation for doin' that to men – givin' 'em perspective." He let Turner's hand go.

"I haven't decided yet."

"Then let me tell you." The surprised look on Turner's face didn't stop Slaughter. "You're a fighter. You're a man who will stand where another won't. You're a Yankee, through and through. Smart fella, too. The war's over, but a new one might just be startin'. I don't want it. Life ain't about bringin' some ideal back to life. Hell, it ain't even about tomorrow. All we got is today. And today, I tell you you're goin' to go find someplace where they need you to stand up and be heard. If a war's comin', today's the perfect day to stop it. Probably tomorrow too. But don't worry about that yet." Clum and Turner stared at the man, fully aware that those were likely the most words he'd said at one time, ever. "Got a place to go?"

For a moment, Turner didn't answer. A moment only. "Yes, sir, I do."

"Then get the hell out of here and go take care of things. You're wastin' time here." With that, Texas John Slaughter nodded and walked out of the doctor's office.

"Well …" Clum pursed his lips for a minute, not sure what to say. "Is he right? Do you have somewhere to go?"

"I do. I'll need to send a telegram first."

"I can help you with that. Get dressed, Turner, and we'll get that message sent."

No one warned Turner how difficult or uncomfortable the simplest of tasks would be, but he managed to pull on the new clothes. Slaughter had left fifty dollars in the bag: Clum had stuffed twenty into the pocket of the trousers. They would be horrified if not insulted should he mention it, certainly if he refused it.

There were too many unanswered questions and a military force preparing to bring war to his country. He couldn't fight them alone. Sherman had noted it: he'd been a loner for too long. That would have to change. The Prussians – Admiral Hagan and Madame – they too were still out there, preparing in the dark, things he hadn't yet imagined.

Already he could hear workmen pounding nails into building frames. Tombstone wouldn't wait to rebuild. Anxiously, people rushed from place to place, complaining, calling out, whistling. He let them pass by. His mind was caught between euphoria of the bright blue desert sky and what his telegram would have to say.

Gabriel waved at him, and quickly crossed the street. "I am told you might be heading east. Now that I have accomplished what I need to, I should go home. As it happens, Monsieur, we are going the same direction."

"Have you accomplished what you meant to?" Turner pulled a new cheroot out of its pouch and offered the others to Gabriel.

"I think so. On the way home, perhaps you can give me details and we shall design a dignified telling of Captain Robur's tale."

"And you will publish it?"

"Yes. And you will send a copy to Doctor Gantry, won't you? If not, I will. But I think she will want it from you."

Slowly Turner lit the sweet tobacco roll. "She might do better without me bothering her."

"Nonsense. Take it from a Frenchman. If she is graced enough to have you and your *amour*, she is better off."

Turner took the cheroot out of his mouth and began to protest such assumptions. There were no logical arguments to be made. Gabriel was right. Then again, he might not be fully aware of the dangers Turner could bring to Lettie by simply *knowing* her. Slaughter's words, "don't worry about that yet," stayed with him. One day at a time. Think it through.

"Are you packed, Monsieur Turner?"

"I am. Come along Monsieur Verne."

Gabriel jumped slightly. "Monsieur Turner?"

"I'll need to stop at the Epitaph office to send a telegram to a general at the Army Headquarters, St. Louis. Otherwise, we catch the stage to Bisbee ..."

Turner looked out at the sweep of the mesas, the desert leading up to the mountains, wanting to remember the beautiful landscape for years to come. Closing his eyes, he smelled the crisp air, burnt wood, dry soil and linked it all to his memory of the place. He didn't look at the French fellow who was clearly taken off guard. "Come along, Monsieur Jules Gabriel Verne. Shall we write the remarkable adventures of a brilliant but mad genius? Let's do him and ourselves a little justice."

COMING
SOON

Don't Miss the Continuing Adventures of
Dr. Lettie Gantry
In

THE VOLCANO
LADY –
VOLUME 3:

THE GREAT
EARTHQUAKE MACHINE

ABOUT THE AUTHOR

T. E. MacArthur is an author, artist, and historian living in the San Francisco Bay Area with her constant companion, Mac the cat. She received her Bachelor's Degree in History from Cal State University and spent many an evening in subsequent Anthropology, Geology, Criminal Investigation and Art classes. Writing, however, remains her passion. She has written for several local and specialized publications and was even an accidental sports reporter for Reuters with three national bi-lines.

The Volcano Lady: Volumes I & II follow the adventures of Victorian lady scientist Lettie Gantry. *The Yankee Must Die* novellas continue the thrilling adventures of Tom Turner following the time honored cliffhangers of dime novels, penny dreadfuls, and weekly serials. To put it mildly, T.E. has a love for all things Victorian (history and clothing from 1870 – 1890 in particular) and is having a lifelong affair with the writings of Jules Verne.

VISIT T. E. MACARTHUR ON HER BLOG:
http://volcanolady1.wordpress.com

OR ON FACEBOOK:
https://www.facebook.com/pages/The-Volcano-Lady-by-TE-MacArthur

www.ingramcontent.com/pod-product-compliance
Lightning Source LLC
Chambersburg PA
CBHW030615130626
46552CB00002B/569